THE **PENGUIN RAY** LIBRARY

SATYAJIT RAY

FELUDA IN THE GOLDEN FORTRESS

Edited by Sandip Ray

Co-edited by Riddhi Goswami

Layout and design by Pinaki De

THE **PENGUIN RAY** LIBRARY

VINTAGE

An imprint of Penguin Random House

VINTAGE

Vintage is an imprint of the Penguin Random House group of companies
whose addresses can be found at global.penguinrandomhouse.com

Published by Penguin Random House India Pvt. Ltd
4th Floor, Capital Tower 1, MG Road,
Gurugram 122 002, Haryana, India

This edition published in Vintage by Penguin Random House India 2024
In association with the Society for the Preservation of Satyajit Ray Archives

Vector illustration of Satyajit Ray's portrait on half-title page by Pinaki De

10 9 8 7 6 5 4 3 2 1

ISBN 9780143456568

Cover illustration by Satyajit Ray
Cover design and book layout by Pinaki De

Printed at Thomson Press India Ltd, New Delhi

www.penguin.co.in

CONTENTS

FOREWORD

When the first Feluda film *Sonar Kella* (*The Golden Fortress*) was released in 1974, I was twenty-one years old. Fifty years since, fond memories from the outdoor shoot of the film are still fresh in my mind. Like most of his films, *Baba* (my father, Satyajit Ray) did a lot of groundwork even before the start of the proper production process. It helped that the basic story was also written by Baba three years ago and published as a novel in 1971. He was planning to do a film exclusively set in Rajasthan for a long time. Earlier, while filming for *Goopy Gyne Bagha Byne* in 1969, he went there for location hunting. Parts of *Goopy Gyne Bagha Byne* are shot in Rajasthan but he wanted to explore the locales more extensively. During that time, most Bengalis would equate Rajasthan with specific touristy destinations like Jaipur, Jodhpur Udaipur or Bikaner. The breathtaking beauty of Jaisalmer was relatively unknown to the average Bengali who was Ray's primary target audience. Today they go to Jaisalmer in order to relive the memories around the locations seen in the film. Old local guides still fondly remember the shoot. There is a even a 'Mukul Stone Shop' within the ramparts of the fort.

The romanticism around the setting has made it the most loved Feluda film. Although Baba made another brilliant Feluda film, *Joi Baba Felunath* (*The Elephant God*), later in 1979, *Sonar Kella* remains the perennial favourite. It is interesting to note that *Baba* changed the cover of the book in the later editions after the film was released, and that bears testimony to the popularity of the film. It is something that he didn't do in the case of *Joi Baba Felunath.* This book contains numerous sketches and other preparatory materials that were made in the run-up to the film. Now the film is also restored and successfully streaming on popular OTT platform with proper subtitles. This book will be a good companion to the younger generation who will hopefully discover the magic of the film.

I am thankful to Riddhi Goswami for co-editing the work and Pinaki De for taking care of the overall design of the book, including the layout. The book would not have been possible without Premanka Goswami, Associate Publisher, Penguin Random House India, whose dedication and enthusiasm to the project ensured that we publish this book just in time to commemorate fifty years of the film.

Kolkata 2024

SANDIP RAY

I. THE STORY

THE GOLDEN FORTRESS

First published as a Bengali novel 'Sonar Kella' in *Desh* Puja Number 1971.
Published as a book by Ananda Publishers in the same year.

Translated from the Bengali by Gopa Majumdar

ONE

Feluda stopped reading and shut his book with a bang. Then he snapped his fingers twice, yawned heavily and said, 'Geometry.'

I asked, 'Were you reading a book on geometry all this while?'

The book was covered with newspaper, so I could not see its title. All I knew was that Feluda had borrowed it from Uncle Sidhu, who was passionate about books. He bought quite a few, and took great care of them. In fact, he did not like lending his books to anyone, but Feluda was an exception. Feluda knew it, so he always put a protective cover on any book that he brought from Uncle Sidhu's house.

Feluda lit a Charminar and blew out two smoke rings, one after the other. 'There is no such thing as a book on geometry,' he told me. 'Any book may be seen as one because everything around us is related to geometry. Did you see those smoke rings? When they left my mouth, they were perfect circles. Now just think. There are circles everywhere. Look at your own body. The iris in your eye is a circle. With the help of the iris, you can look at the sun and the moon. If you think of them as flat objects, they are circles, but of course they are actually spheres—each a solid bubble. That's geometry. The planets in the solar system are orbiting the sun in elliptic curves. There's geometry again. When you spat out of the window a little while ago—you shouldn't have done that, it's most unhygienic and if you do it again, you'll get a sharp rap on the head, but anyway—that spit went out in a parabolic curve. Geometry, see? Have you ever looked at a spider's web in any detail? It starts with a simple square. Then two diagonal lines run through it and the square is divided into four triangles. After that, the spider starts weaving a spiral web from the intersecting point of those diagonal lines. That keeps growing in size, until it covers the entire square. If you think about it, your head will start reeling...it's something so amazing!'

It was a Sunday morning. The two of us were sitting in our living room on the ground floor. Baba had gone to visit his childhood friend, Subimal, as he did every Sunday. Feluda was seated on a sofa, his feet resting on a low table.

I was on a divan, leaning on a cushion placed against the wall. In my hand was a game. It was a maze, made of plastic. Inside the maze were tiny metal balls. Over the last half hour, I had been trying to make those metal balls slip through the various lanes in the maze and go straight to its centre. Now I realized that the game was a matter of complex geometry, too.

A Durga Puja was being held in Nihar and Pintu's house, which was near ours. Someone was playing a song over a loudspeaker—*Yeh jo muhabbat hai* from the film *Kati Patang*. Fine spiral grooves on a circular record. More geometry!

'Geometry applies not just to objects you can see,' Feluda continued. 'The human mind often follows geometric patterns. A simple man's mind will run along a straight line. Others who are not so simple may have minds that twist and wriggle like a snake. And the mind of a lunatic? No one can tell how that's going to run. It's a matter of the most convoluted geometry!'

Thanks to Feluda, I had come across plenty of people from every category. What kind of geometric pattern did he fall into? When I asked him, Feluda said, 'You might call me a many-pointed star.'

'And I? Am I a satellite of that star?'

'You are merely a point, something that indicates a position, but has no significance of its own.'

I like to think of myself as a satellite. The only problem is that I cannot play that role all the time. I managed to be with Feluda when we had trouble in Gangtok because that was during school holidays. Two cases had followed—one was a murder in Dhalbhoomgarh, and the other was to do with a forged will in Patna—which I missed altogether. Now my school was closed once again for Puja. I was wondering if a new case would come along. Who knew whether it really would? But then, Feluda did tell me that if one badly wants something to happen, and if one's will is strong enough, then a particular wish may well come true, more or less automatically. I quite like to think what happened that Sunday morning was simply a result of my willing it.

A song from the film *Johnny Mera Naam* had just started on the loudspeaker; Feluda had flicked a quantity of ash into an ashtray and picked up the *Hindustan Standard*; I was toying with the idea of going out, when someone rattled the knocker on our door very loudly. Baba, I knew, would not be back before twelve o'clock. This had to be someone else. I opened the door and found a simple, mild looking man, wearing a dhoti and a blue shirt.

'Does a Pradosh Mitter live in this house?' he asked, raising his voice to make himself heard. The loudspeaker was making quite a racket.

Feluda rose from the sofa and came to the door on hearing his name. 'Where have you come from?' he asked.

'All the way from Shyambazar,' the man replied.

'Please come in.'

The man stepped into the living room.

'Please sit down. I am Pradosh Mitter.'

'Oh. Oh, I see. I didn't know…I mean, I didn't realize you were so young!' The man sat down on a chair next to the sofa, looking visibly impressed. But the smile on his face disappeared almost at once.

'What can I do for you?' Feluda asked.

The man cleared his throat. 'I have heard a lot about you from Kailash Chowdhury. He seems to think very highly of you. He…he is one of my customers, you see. My name is Sudhir Dhar. I have a book shop in College Street—Dhar & Co. You may have seen it.'

Feluda nodded briefly, before saying to me, 'Topshe, please shut that window.'

I shut the window that overlooked the street. That reduced the noise, and Mr Dhar could then speak normally.

'About a week ago, there was a press report about my son. Did you…?'

'Press report? What did it say?'

'About his being a *jatismar*…I mean…'

'About a boy called Mukul?'

'Yes.'

'So the report's true?'

'You see, from the way he speaks, the kind of things he says, it does seem as if…' Mr Dhar broke off.

I knew what the word *jatismar* meant. A person who can recall events from a previous life is called a *jatismar*. Apparently, there are people who get periodic flashes of memory related to a life that they had lived long before they were born in their present incarnation. Mind you, even Feluda does not know whether or not there is any truth behind this whole business.

Feluda picked up the packet of Charminar and offered it to Mr Dhar, who smiled and shook his head. Then he said, 'Perhaps you remember what my son told the reporter? He's only eight, but he described a place which he is supposed to have seen. Yet I am sure nobody from Ray family—not even my forefathers—has been there, let alone my son. We are very ordinary people, you see. I only have that shop, and the book trade these days is…'

'Doesn't your son talk of a fortress?' Feluda interrupted him.

'Yes, that's right. A golden fortress. There was a cannon on its roof, a lot of fighting, and several people were killed…my son says he has seen it all. He used to wear a turban and ride a camel on the sand. He mentions sand quite frequently. And animals—camels, elephants and horses. Oh, and peacocks. There is a mark near his elbow. We always thought it was a birthmark, but he says he was once attacked by a peacock, and the mark shows where the bird pecked him.'

'Has he ever mentioned exactly where he used to live?'

'No, but he does say that he could see this golden fortress from his house. Sometimes he draws funny squiggles with a pencil and says, "Look, that's my house!" If you look at it, well yes, it does appear to be a house.'

'Could he not have seen all that in a book? I mean, you have a book shop, don't you? So maybe he saw pictures of this place in a book?'

'Yes, that's a possibility. But other children also look at pictures in books; they don't talk incessantly about what they've seen, do they? If you'd seen my son, you'd know what I mean. To tell you the truth, his mind seems to be elsewhere. His own family—his parents, brothers and sisters, other relatives—no one seems to matter to him. In fact, he doesn't even look at us when he talks.'

'When did this whole thing start?'

'About two months ago. It started with those pictures, you see. One day, when I got back home from the shop—it had rained a lot that day—my son began showing me the pictures he had drawn. At first, I paid him no attention. Every child likes talking about imaginary lands, and he was chattering away. So I ignored him. It was my wife who first noticed that there was something odd. Then we listened more carefully to his words, and watched his behaviour over the next few weeks…then, one of my other customers, Dr Hemanga Hajra…have you heard of him?'

'Yes, yes. He's a parapsychologist, isn't he? I've certainly heard of him. But didn't that press report say he was going to travel somewhere with your son?'

'Not going to. Has gone. They've already left. Dr Hajra came to my house three times. He thought Mukul was talking of Rajasthan. So I said, yes, that could be true. Then, in the end, Dr Hajra told me he was doing research on this whole business of recalling a previous life. He wanted to take Mukul to Rajputana. He thought that if Mukul could actually go back to the same place, he might remember several other things, and that would help his research. So he said he'd pay for everything, and take great care of my son, I wouldn't have to worry.'

'And then?' Feluda leaned forward. His voice had changed. Clearly, he was finding all this quite interesting.

'Then they left, that's all.'

'Didn't Mukul mind leaving home?'

Mr Dhar smiled a little wanly. 'Mind? Oh no. He was ready to go with Dr Hajra the minute he offered to show him the golden fortress. My son, you see, is not like other children. He's very different. We find him awake at three in the morning sometimes. He'd be humming a song. Not any film song, mind you. Something like a folk song, like the kind of music you hear in villages—but certainly it doesn't come from any village in Bengal. That much I can tell you. I know a little about music…I play the harmonium, you see.'

Mr Dhar had told us a lot about his son. But he had said nothing about why he had come to see Feluda, or why he needed to consult a detective. Feluda's next question made the whole conversation take a different turn.

'Didn't your son say something about hidden treasure?'

Mr Dhar began to look even more depressed. 'That is the biggest problem!' he sighed. 'He told me about it some time ago, but when he mentioned it to the reporter… well, that proved disastrous!'

Feluda did not reply. He was lost in thought; four deep lines had appeared on his forehead.

'Why do you say that?' Feluda asked. Then he called out to our cook Srinath, and told him to bring tea.

'Let me explain,' Mr Dhar continued. 'Dr Hajra left for Rajasthan with Mukul yesterday morning by the Toofan Express. And...'

'Do you know where in Rajasthan he'll go?' Feluda interrupted.

'Jodhpur, so he said. Since Mukul had mentioned sand, he said he'd start with the northwest. Anyway, what happened was that yesterday evening, someone kidnapped a boy from our area. He was about Mukul's age.'

'And you think that boy was kidnapped by mistake? Because they thought he was Mukul?'

'Yes, there is no question about that. My son and this other boy happen to look similar. The other boy is Shivratan Mukherjee's grandson. Mr Mukherjee is one of our neighbours, he's a solicitor. The boy is called Neelu. They were naturally most upset, had to call the police, and there was an enormous fuss, as you can imagine. But now that they've got him back, things have calmed down.'

'Got him back? Already?'

'Early this morning. But how does that make any difference, tell me? I am going mad with anxiety, I tell you. Those kidnappers obviously realized they got the wrong boy. And Neelu has told them that Mukul has gone to Jodhpur. Suppose they chase Mukul all the way to Jodhpur just to lay their hands on that treasure?'

Feluda did not reply. He was lost in thought; four deep lines had appeared on his forehead. My heart was beating faster. Could it mean that we'd go to Rajasthan during these Puja holidays? Jodhpur, Chittor, Udaipur...I had only heard these names and read about these places in history books—and, of course, in *Raj Kahini* by Abanindranath Tagore. Uncle Naresh had given me a copy on my birthday.

Srinath came in with the tea. He placed the tray on a table. Feluda offered a cup to Mr Dhar.

'From what I heard about you from Kailash Chowdhury,' Mr Dhar began hesitantly, 'it appears that you were most...er...I mean...anyway, I was just wondering if you might be able to go to Rajasthan. If you found that Dr Hajra and Mukul were safe, that's well and good. But suppose they were in danger? Suppose you saw something odd? I mean, I've heard that you're brave, you'd tackle criminals. I am only an ordinary man, Mr Mitter. Perhaps it is impertinent of me to have come to you. But...if you did decide to go, I would certainly pay for your travel.'

Feluda continued to frown. After a minute's silence, he said, 'I shall let you know tomorrow what I decide. I assume you have got a photo of your son in your house? The one printed in the newspaper was not very clear.'

Mr Dhar took a long sip of his tea. 'My cousin is fond of photography. He took some photos of Mukul. My wife will have them.'

'Very well.'

Mr Dhar finished his tea, put the cup down on a table and rose. 'I have a telephone in my shop, 345116. I am usually in the shop from ten o'clock.'

'Where do you live?'

'Mechhobazar. 7 Mechhobazar Street. My house is on the main road.'

I went with Mr Dhar to see him out. When he'd gone, I shut the front door and returned to the living room. 'There's one word that I didn't quite understand,' I said to Feluda.

'You mean parapsychologist?'

'Yes.'

'Those who study certain hazy aspects of the human mind are called parapsychologists. Take telepathy, for instance. You can actually get into the mind of another person and read their thoughts. Or, if your own mind is strong enough, you can influence other people's thoughts, even change them totally. Strange things happen sometimes. Suppose you were sitting here, thinking of an old friend. Suddenly, out of the blue, the same friend rang you. A parapsychologist would tell you that there was nothing sudden or unexpected about it. If your friend rang you, it was because of strong telepathy. But there is more—like extra-sensory perception, or ESP for short. It can warn you about future events. Or, for that matter, take this business of recalling a previous life. All these could be subjects a parapsychologist might wish to study.'

'Is this Hemanga Hajra a famous parapsychologist?'

'Yes, one of the best known. He's been abroad, given lectures, and I think even formed a society.'

'Do you believe in such things?'

'What I believe is simply that it is foolish to accept or reject anything without sufficient evidence. If you don't keep an open mind, you're a fool. One look at history would show you plenty of examples of such stupidity. There was a time when some people thought that the earth was flat. Did you know that? They also thought that the earth came to an end at one particular point, and you couldn't travel beyond that. But when the navigator Magellan began his journey round the world from one place and returned to the same spot, all those who thought the earth was flat began scratching their heads. Then there have been people who thought the earth was fixed, and other planets, even the sun, moved around it. Some thought the sky was like a huge bowl turned upside down. All the stars were fixed on it like jewels, they thought. It was Copernicus who proved that the sun remained stationary, and the earth and other planets in the solar system orbited the sun. But Copernicus thought this movement followed a circular motion. Then Kepler came along and proved that everything moved in elliptic curves. After that, Galileo...but anyway, there's no point in talking about all that. Your mind is too young, and too immature to grasp such things!'

Clever detective though he was, Feluda did not seem to realize one simple thing. None of his jibes and jeers was going to spoil my excitement because my heart was already telling me that the holidays were going to be spent in Rajasthan. We would see a new place, and unravel a new mystery. What remained to be tested was the strength of my own telepathy.

TWO

Feluda had told Mr Dhar that he would take a day to make up his mind. But within an hour of Mr Dhar's departure, he decided that he would go to Rajasthan. When he told me about it, I asked, 'I am going with you, aren't I?'

'If you can name five places in Rajasthan that have forts—all within a minute—then you might stand a chance.'

'Jodhpur, Jaipur, Chittor, Bikaner and . . . and . . . Bundi!'

Feluda glanced at his watch and sprang to his feet. It took him exactly three and a half minutes to change from a kurta pyjama into a shirt and trousers. 'It's Sunday, so Fairlie Place will stay open till twelve o'clock. Let me go quickly and make our reservations,' he said.

It was one o'clock by the time Feluda returned. The first thing he did upon his return was to look up Hemanga Hajra's phone number in the directory and ring him. When I asked him why he was calling someone who was out of town, Feluda said, 'I needed proof that what Mr Dhar told us was true.'

'And did you get it?'

'Yes.'

After lunch, Feluda spent the whole afternoon stretched on his bed, a pillow tucked under his chest, going through five different books. Two of them were Pelican books on parapsychology. Feluda said he had borrowed them from a friend. Of the others, one was Todd's book on Rajasthan, the second was called *A Guide to India*, *Pakistan, Burma and Ceylon*, and the third was a book on Indian history, but I can't remember who wrote it.

In the evening, when we'd had our tea, Feluda said, 'Get ready, we're going out. We need to visit Mr Dhar.'

By this time, I had told Baba about our plans. He was very pleased to hear that we were going to Rajasthan. He had been there twice in his childhood with my grandfather. 'Don't miss Chittor,' he told me. 'The fort in Chittor is quite awe-inspiring. It's easy enough to guess what made the Rajputs such brave warriors.'

We arrived at Mr Dhar's house at around half past six. When he heard that Feluda was prepared to go to Rajasthan, Mr Dhar looked both relieved and grateful. 'I do not know how to thank you!' he exclaimed.

'It isn't yet time to start thanking me, Mr Dhar. You must assume that we are going purely as tourists, not because you asked us to. Anyway, we have very little time. There are two things we need. One is a photo of your son. The other is a chat with Neelu, that boy who was kidnapped.'

'Let me see what I can do. Usually, Neelu is never at home in the evenings, especially now that Puja is round the corner. But I don't think that today he'll be allowed to go out on his own. Wait, I'll get that photo.'

Shivratan Mukherjee, the solicitor, lived only three houses away, on the same side of the road. We found him at home, having a cup of tea in his living room with another gentleman. Mr Mukherjee's visitor seemed to have a skin disease—there were white patches on his face. When Mr Dhar explained why we were there, Mr Mukherjee remarked, 'My grandson seems to have become quite famous, thanks to your son! Please sit down. Manohar!'

Manohar turned out to be his servant. 'Bring more tea,' Mr Mukherjee told him, 'and see if you can find Neelu. Tell him I've sent for him.'

We found ourselves three chairs placed by the side of a large table. The walls on both sides were covered by very tall bookcases, almost reaching the ceiling. They were crammed with fat tomes. Feluda had once told me that no one needed to consult books as much as a lawyer.

While we were waiting for Neelu, I had a look at Mukul's photo. It had been taken on their roof. The little boy was standing in the sun, frowning straight at the camera. There was no smile on his face.

Mr Mukherjee said, 'We asked Neelu a lot of questions, too. At first, he was in such a state of shock that he wasn't talking at all. Now he appears more normal.'

'Have the police been told?' Feluda asked.

'Yes, we told the police when he went missing. But he came back before the police could do anything.'

The servant returned with Neelu. Mr Dhar was right. Neelu did bear a strong resemblance to the boy in the photo. He looked at us suspiciously. Clearly, he had not yet got over his ordeal.

Suddenly, Feluda asked him, 'Did you hurt your hand, Neelu?'

Mr Mukherjee opened his mouth to say something, but Feluda made a gesture and stopped him. Neelu answered the question himself. 'When they pulled my hand, it burned a lot.'

There was a cut over his wrist, clearly visible.

'They? You mean there was more than one person?'

'One man covered my eyes and my mouth. Then he picked me up and put me in a car. Another man drove the car. I felt very scared.'

'So would I,' Feluda told him. 'In fact, I would have felt much more scared than you. You are very brave. When they caught you, what were you doing?'

'I was going to Moti's house. They have a Durga Puja in their house. I wanted to see the idol. Moti is in my class.'

'Was it very quiet in the streets? Not many people about?'

'The day before yesterday,' Mr Mukherjee informed us, 'we had some trouble here. A bomb went off. So, since last evening, there have been fewer people out in the streets.'

Feluda nodded and said, 'Hmm.' Then he turned to Neelu once more. 'Where did they take you?'

'I don't know. They tied a cloth over my eyes. The car drove on and on.'

'And then?'

'Then they made me sit in a chair. One of them said, "Which school do you go to?" I told him. Then he said, "We're going to ask you a few questions. Tell us exactly what you know. If you do, we'll drop you in front of your school. Can you go home from there?" So I said, "Yes." Then I said, "You must hurry, my mother will scold me if I get late!" Then he said, "Where is the golden fortress?" I said, "I don't know, and nor does Mukul. He only knows there's a fort, that's all." Then the two men began talking with each other in English. I heard them say, "Mistake!" One man said to me, "What's your name?" I said, "Mukul's my friend, but he's gone to Rajasthan." He said, "Do you know where in Rajasthan he's gone?" I told him, "Jaipur!"'

'Then the two men began talking with each other in English. I heard them say, "Mistake!"'

'You said Jaipur?' Feluda asked him.

'N-no, no. Jodhpur. Yes, that's what I said. Jodhpur.'

Neelu stopped. All of us remained silent. The servant had placed tea and sweets before us, but no one seemed interested in them.

'Can you think of anything else?' Feluda prompted Neelu.

Neelu thought for a minute. Then he said, 'One of them was smoking a cigarette. No, no, it was a cigar.'

'Do you know how a cigar smells?'

'Yes, my uncle smokes them.'

'All right. Where did you sleep at night?'

'I don't know.'

'You don't know? What do you mean?'

'Well, they said, "Here's some milk. Drink it." Then someone handed me a very heavy glass. I drank the milk, then fell asleep. I was still sitting in the chair!'

'And then? When you woke up?'

Neelu looked uncertainly at his grandfather. Mr Mukherjee smiled. 'He woke up only after he was brought home,' he explained. 'They left him outside his school, possibly very early this morning. He was still asleep. The man who delivers our newspaper every day happened to be passing by a little later, and saw him. It was he who came and told us. Then I went with my son and brought him back. Our doctor has seen him. He said Neelu was given a sleeping draught—probably a heavier dose than what might normally be given to a child.'

Feluda looked grave. He picked up his cup of tea and muttered under his breath, 'Scoundrels!' Then, he patted Neelu's back and said, 'Thank you, Neelu Babu. You may go now.'

When we had said goodbye to Mr Mukherjee and were out in the street once more, Mr Dhar asked, 'Do you think there's reason for concern?'

'What I can see is that some greedy and reckless people have become unduly curious about your son. What's difficult to say is whether they'll really go all the way to Rajasthan. By the way, I think you should write to Dr Hajra, just to introduce me. After all, he doesn't know me. So if I can show him your letter, it will help.'

Mr Dhar wrote the letter, handed it to Feluda and offered to pay for our travel once more. Feluda paid no attention. As we approached our bus stop, Mr Dhar said, 'Please let me know, sir, when you get there and find them. I'll be ever so worried. Dr Hajra has promised to write as well. But even if he doesn't, you must…at least one letter…!'

On reaching home, Feluda took out his famous blue notebook (volume six) before either of us began packing. Then he sat down on his bed and said, 'Let's get some dates sorted out. When did Dr Hajra leave with Mukul to go to Rajasthan?'

'Yesterday, 9 October.'

'When was Neelu kidnapped?'

'Yesterday, in the evening.'

'And he returned this morning, that's 10 October. We are leaving tomorrow morning, the 11th. We'll reach Agra on the 12th. Then we'll have to change trains there, and catch one in the evening that goes to Bandikui. Leave Bandikui at midnight, and reach Marwar the same day...that'll be the 13th evening...13th...13th...'

Feluda continued to mutter and did some funny calculations. Then he said, 'Geometry. Even here you'll find geometry. A single point...and there are various lines converging to meet that point. Geometry!'

THREE

Half an hour ago, we boarded a train at the Agra Fort station to go to Bandikui. We had about three hours to kill in Agra. So we went to see the Taj Mahal again—after ten years—and Feluda gave me a short lecture on the geometry of the building.

Yesterday, before leaving Calcutta, we had to attend to some important business. Perhaps I should mention it here. Since the Toofan Express left at 9.30 in the morning, we were both up quite early. At around six o'clock, after we'd had tea, Feluda said, 'We ought to visit Uncle Sidhu before we go. If he can give us some information, it will really help.'

Uncle Sidhu lives in Sardar Shankar Road, which is only five minutes from our Tara Road. Uncle Sidhu is a strange character. He spent most of his life doing various kinds of businesses, earning a lot of money, and then losing much of it. Now he has retired. His main passion is books. He buys them in large numbers, and spends some of his time on reading, and the rest on playing chess all by himself. Sometimes, he consults a book on chess in between making moves.

His other passion is food—or rather, experimenting with food. He likes mixing one item with another. According to him, yoghurt mixed with an omelette tastes like ambrosia. To tell the truth, he is not related to us. He used to live next door to us back in our ancestral village (which I have never seen). So he's like an elder brother to my father, and we call him 'uncle'.

When we reached his house, he was seated on a low stool, blocking the entrance through his front door, and having his hair cut by his barber, although he has no hair except for some around the back of his head. Upon seeing us, he moved his stool a little and allowed us to go through. 'Make yourselves comfortable,' he said. 'Yell for Narayan, he'll give you some tea.'

Uncle Sidhu's room was very simply furnished. There was only a divan, two chairs and three very large bookcases. Books covered half the divan. We knew that the little empty space on it was where Uncle Sidhu liked to sit, so we took the two chairs. Feluda had remembered to bring the book he'd borrowed, which was still covered with newspaper.

He slipped it back into an empty slot on a shelf.

The barber continued to work on Uncle Sidhu's hair. 'Felu,' said Uncle Sidhu, 'you are a detective. I hope you've read up on the history of criminal investigation? It doesn't matter what you specialize in. If you know something about the history of your profession, you'll gain more confidence and find your work much more interesting.'

'Yes, of course,' Feluda replied politely.

'Who was the first to discover the technique of identifying a criminal through his fingerprints? Can you tell me?'

Feluda winked at me and said, 'I can't remember. I did read about it somewhere, but now. . ..'

I could tell that Feluda knew the answer all right, but was pretending that he didn't, just to please Uncle Sidhu.

'Hmm. Most people would immediately tell you that it was Alphonse Bertillon. But that's wrong. The correct name is Juan Vucatich. Remember that. He was from Argentina. He was the first to emphasize the importance of thumbprints. Then he divided those prints into four categories. A few years later, Henry from England strengthened the system.'

Feluda glanced at his watch and decided to come straight to the point. 'You may have heard of Dr Hemanga Hajra, the parapsychologist—?'

'Certainly,' said Uncle Sidhu, 'Why, I saw his name in the papers only the other day! What's he done? Something fishy? But he's not the kind of man to get mixed up in funny business. On the contrary, he has exposed others . . .cheats and frauds.'

'Really?' Feluda looked up. We were about to hear an interesting story.

'Yes, don't you know about it? It happened about four years ago, and was reported in the press. A Bengali gentleman—no, I should not call him a gentleman, he was actually a scoundrel—started a centre for spiritual healing in Chicago. Bang in the city centre. Clients poured in every day. The Americans have plenty of money, and are easily impressed by new ideas. This Bengali claimed that he could use hypnotism and cure even the most complex diseases. The same sort of thing that Anton Mesmer did in Europe in the eighteenth century. Perhaps the Bengali managed to cure a couple of patients—that's not unusual; a few stray cases would be successful. But, around the same time, Hajra arrived in Chicago on a lecture tour. He went to see things for himself, and caught the man out. Oh God, it was a scandal! In the end, the American government forced him to leave the country. Yes, yes…I can remember his name now…he called himself Bhavananda. That man, Hajra, though, is a solid character. At least, that's the impression one gets from his articles. I've got two of them. See in the right hand corner of that bookcase on your left. You'll find three journals of the Parapsychological Society.'

Feluda borrowed all three journals. Now, sitting on the train, he was leafing through them. I was looking out of the window and watching the scenery. A little while ago, we had left Uttar Pradesh and entered Rajasthan.

'The sun here has a different brilliance. No wonder the men are so powerful!'

These words in Bengali came from the bench opposite us. It was a four-berth compartment, and there were four passengers. The man who had spoken those words looked perfectly meek and mild, was very thin and probably shorter than me by at least two inches. And I was only fifteen, so it was likely that I'd grow taller with time. This man was at least thirty-five; there was no chance that his height would ever change. As he was dressed in a bush shirt and trousers, I had been unable to guess from his clothes that he was another Bengali.

He glanced at Feluda, smiled and said, 'I've been listening to your conversation for a long time. I'm lucky to have found fellow Bengalis so far away from home. In fact, I'd assumed that for a whole month I'd be forced to boycott my mother tongue!'

Feluda asked, possibly purely out of politeness, 'Are you going far?'

'Up to Jodhpur. Then I'll decide where else I might go. What about yourselves?'

'We are going to Jodhpur, too.'

'Oh, wonderful. Are you also a writer?'

'Oh no,' Feluda smiled, 'I am only a reader. Do you write?'

'Are you familiar with the name of Jatayu?'

'Jatayu?' I asked. 'The writer of all those thrillers?' I had read one or two of his books—*Shivers in the Sahara* and *The Ferocious Foe*. I had borrowed them from our school library.

'You are Jatayu?' Feluda asked.

'Yes, sir,' the man flashed his teeth, his head bent in a bow. 'I am Jatayu. At your service. I write under that pseudonym. Namaskar.'

'Namaskar. My name is Pradosh Mitter. And this is Sreeman Tapeshranjan.'

How could Feluda keep a straight face? I could feel laughter bubbling up inside me, threatening to burst forth. This was Jatayu?

And I used to think a writer who could write such tales would have looks to match—perhaps even James Bond would be put in the shade!

'My real name is Lalmohan Ganguli. But please don't tell anyone. A pseudonym—like a disguise—must never be revealed. I mean, if it is, then it loses its impact, don't you think?'

We had bought a packet of sweet gulabi rewri in Agra. Feluda offered the packet to Jatayu and said, 'You seem to have been on the move for some time!'

'Yes, that's...' Jatayu picked up a rewri and suddenly broke off, looking a bit confused. Then he threw a startled glance at Feluda and asked, 'How can you tell?'

Feluda smiled. 'The strap on your wristwatch slips at times. When it does, it exposes the only part of your arm that isn't sunburnt.'

Jatayu's eyes grew round. 'Oh my God, what terrific powers of observation you have got! Yes, you're right. I left home about ten days ago, and travelled to Delhi, Agra and Fatehpur Sikri. So far, I've only written about adventures in foreign lands.

'I live in Bhadreshwar. So I thought I should travel a bit, see new places, it would help me in my writing. Besides, these areas are much better suited to adventure stories, aren't they? Look at those barren hills, rising high like biceps and triceps. Our Bengal has no muscles— except, of course, for the Himalayas. You can't have a successful adventure on the plains!'

The three of us continued to eat the rewri. Then I caught Jatayu casting sidelong glances at Feluda. Finally, he asked, 'What is your height? Please don't mind my asking.'

'Nearly six feet,' Feluda replied.

'Oh, that's a very good height, the same as my hero's. Prakhar Rudra—you do know his name, don't you? Prakhar is a Russian name, but it suits a Bengali, too, don't you think? The thing is, you see, I've got my hero to be everything I could never be myself. God knows I tried hard enough. When I was in college, I saw advertisements of Charles Atlas in British magazines. There he was, standing proudly, his chest and all his muscles expanded, his hands on his waist. He looked like a lion! There was not even an ounce of fat on his body. His muscles rippled like waves, from head to toe. And the advertisement said, "If you follow my system, you will look like me within a month!" Well, that may be true of Europeans. In Bengal, that kind of thing is impossible. My father was well off, so I wasted some of his money, sent for their lessons and followed them religiously.

'Nothing happened. I remained just the same. Then an uncle said, "Try swinging from a curtain rod. You'll grow taller in a month." A month? For several months, I swung from a rod until, one day, it came off and I fell down. That dislocated my knee, but my height remained stuck at five feet and three-and-half inches. That told me plainly that even if I were pulled in different directions by two teams—as they do in a tug-of-war—I would never grow any taller. So, eventually, I thought enough was enough. There was no point in thinking about the muscles in my body. I decided to pay more attention to the muscles in my brain. And increase my mental height. I began writing thrillers. But I knew Lalmohan Ganguli was not a name that would help sell books. So I took a pseudonym. Jatayu. A fighter. Just think of the fight he put up with Ravan!'

Although our train was called a 'fast passenger', it was stopping at so many stations that it was not able to run for more than twenty minutes at a stretch. Feluda left the journals on parapsychology and began reading a book on Rajasthan. It had pictures of all the forts.

Feluda was looking at those very carefully and reading the descriptions.

On the upper berth opposite us was a man whose moustache and clothes proclaimed clearly that he was not a Bengali. He was eating oranges—one after another—and collecting the peel and other debris on a sheet of a Urdu newspaper spread in front of him.

Feluda was marking a few places in his book with a blue pencil, when Lalmohan Babu said, 'May I ask you something? Are you a detective?'

'Why do you ask?'

'No, I mean...you could tell so easily about my travelling!'

'Well, I am interested in that kind of thing.'

'Good. You're also going to Jodhpur, didn't you say?'

'Yes.'

'In connection with a mystery? If so, I am going to join you...I mean, if you don't mind, that is. I'll never get such a chance again.'

'I hope you wouldn't object to riding a camel?'

'A camel? Oh my God!' Lalmohan Babu's eyes began to glint. 'Ship of the desert! It's always been my dream. I have written about Bedouins in one of my novels—*Bloodbath in Arabia.* And I've mentioned camels in *Shivers in the Sahara.* It's a fascinating creature. Just picture the scene. An entire row of camels, travelling through an ocean of sand, mile after mile, carrying their own water supply in their intestines. How romantic—oh!'

'Er…when you wrote your novel, did you mention that bit about the intestines?'

Lalmohan Babu began looking uncertain. 'Why, is that incorrect?'

Feluda nodded. 'Yes. You see, the source of the water is actually in a camel's hump. The hump is really an accumulation of fat. A camel can oxidize that fat and turn it into water. So it can survive without drinking any water for ten to fifteen days. But, once they do find water, camels have been known to drink as much as twenty-five gallons at one go.'

'Thank goodness you told me all this,' said Lalmohan Babu. 'I must correct that mistake in the next edition.'

FOUR

The train was slow, but at least it wasn't running significantly late. When one has to take connecting trains, it can cause great problems if the first train is delayed.

We saw the first peacocks on reaching Bharatpur. Opposite our platform, there were three of them roaming freely on the tracks. Feluda said to me, 'You will find that peacocks and parrots are as common here as crows and sparrows in Calcutta.'

All the men we saw had turbans on their heads and sideburns on their cheeks—the size of which seemed to be getting larger as we travelled. They were all Rajasthanis, wearing short dhotis which reached their knees, and shirts with buttons on one side. On their feet were heavy naagras. Most men were carrying stout sticks in their hands.

We went to the refreshment room in the station in Bandikui to have dinner. Tucking into his roti and meat curry, Lalmohan Babu remarked, 'See all these men? There's a high probability that some of them are bandits. The Aravalli Hills act as a den for bandits—you know that, don't you? And I'm sure I don't have to tell you how powerful they are. When they are thrown into prison, they can push apart the iron bars on their windows with their bare hands, and escape through the gap!'

'Yes, I know,' Feluda replied. 'And do you know how they punish those who cross them?'

'They're killed, surely?'

'No. That's the beauty of it. If a bandit is annoyed with someone, he will hunt him down—no matter where that person is hiding—and then chop his nose off with a sword. That's all.'

Lalmohan Babu had just picked up a piece of meat. He forgot to put it in his mouth. 'Chop off his nose?' he asked.

'Yes, so I've heard.'

'It sounds most barbaric! Like something straight out of the dark ages. How terrible!'

We caught a train to Marwar in the middle of the night. It did involve scrambling in the dark, but we found enough room for ourselves and slept well.

In the morning, when I woke up, I glanced out of the window and saw an old fort in the distance, on top of a hill. Only a minute later, the train pulled into a station called Kisangarh.

'If you see the word "garh" attached to the name of a place, you may assume that somewhere in that area there is a fort on a hilltop,' Feluda said.

We got down on the platform and had tea. The earthen pots in which the tea was served were much larger and stronger than the pots used in Bengal. Even the tea tasted different. Feluda thought camel's milk had been used. Perhaps that was why Lalmohan Babu ordered a second pot when he finished the first.

When I'd finished mine, I found a tap on the platform and quickly brushed my teeth. Then I splashed cold water on my face and returned to our compartment.

There was a Rajasthani man sitting at one end of Lalmohan Babu's bench. On his head was a huge turban. One leg was folded up on the bench, and he was resting his chin on his raised knee. He had wrapped a shawl around himself, hiding most of his face. But I could see the colour of his shirt through the shawl. It was bright red.

Lalmohan Babu saw the man and promptly abandoned his bench and moved to ours. He tried to huddle in one corner. Feluda said, 'Why don't you two sit more comfortably?' He moved across to the other bench and sat down beside the Rajasthani.

I began to peer more closely at the man's turban. Heaven knew how many twists and turns the fabric had made before it was finally wound so tightly round his head. Lalmohan Babu addressed Feluda and said softly, 'Powerfully suspicious. He is dressed as an ordinary villager, but how come he is in a first-class compartment? Look at that bundle. God knows if it's packed with diamonds and other precious stones.'

The bundle was placed next to the man. Lalmohan Babu's comment made Feluda smile, but he said nothing.

The train started. Feluda took out the book on Rajasthan from his shoulder bag. I took out Newman's Bradshaw timetable and began looking up the stations we would stop at. Each place had a strange name: Galota, Tilonia, Makrera, Vesana, Sendra. Where had these names come from? Feluda had told me once that a lot of local history was always hidden in the name given to a place. But who was going to look for the history behind these

'Powerfully suspicious. He is dressed as an ordinary villager, but how come he is in a first-class compartment?'

names? The train continued to chug on its way. Suddenly, I could feel someone tugging at my shirt. I turned to find that Lalmohan Babu had gone visibly pale. When he caught my eye, he swallowed and whispered, 'Blood!'

Blood? What was the man talking about?

Lalmohan Babu's eyes turned to the Rajasthani. The latter was fast asleep. His head was flung back, his mouth slightly open. My eyes fell on the foot on the bench. The skin around the big toe was badly grazed. It had obviously been bleeding, but now the blood had dried. Then I realized something else. The dark stains on his clothes, which appeared to be mud stains, were, in fact, patches of dried blood.

I looked quickly at Feluda. He was reading his book, quite unconcerned. Lalmohan Babu found his nonchalance too much to bear. He spoke again, in the same choked voice, 'Mr Mitter, suspicious blood marks on our new co-passenger!'

Feluda looked up, glanced once at the Rajasthani and said, 'Probably caused by bugs.'

The thought that the blood was simply the result of bites from bed bugs made Lalmohan Babu look like a pricked balloon. Even so, he could not relax. He continued to sit stiffly and frown and cast the Rajasthani sidelong glances from time to time.

The train reached Marwar Junction at half past two. We had lunch in the refreshment room, and spent almost an hour walking about on the platform. When we climbed into another train at half past three to go to Jodhpur, there was no sign of that Rajasthani wearing a red shirt.

Our journey to Jodhpur lasted for two-and-a-half hours. On the way, we saw several groups of camels. Each time that happened, Lalmohan Babu grew most excited. By the time we reached Jodhpur, it was ten past six. Our train was delayed by twenty minutes. If we were still in Calcutta, the sun would have set by now, but as we were in the western part of the country, it was still shining brightly.

We had booked rooms at the Circuit House. Lalmohan Babu said he would stay at the New Bombay Lodge. 'I'll join you early tomorrow morning, we can all go together to see the fort,' he said and went off towards the tongas that were standing in a row.

We found ourselves a taxi and left the station. The Circuit House wasn't far, we were told. As we drove through the streets, I noticed a huge wall—visible through the gaps between houses—that seemed as high as a two-storeyed house. There was a time, Feluda told me, when the whole of Jodhpur was surrounded by that wall. There were gates in seven different places. If they heard of anyone coming to attack Jodhpur, all seven gates were closed.

Our car went round a bend. Feluda said at once, 'Look, on your left!'

In the far distance, high above all the buildings in the city, stood a sprawling, sombre-looking fort—the famous fort of Jodhpur. Its rulers had once fought for the Mughals.

I was still wondering how soon I'd get to see the fort at close quarters, when we reached the Circuit House. Our taxi passed through the gate, drove up the driveway, past a garden, and stopped under a portico. We got out, collected our luggage and paid the driver.

A gentleman emerged from the building and asked us if we were from Calcutta, and whether Feluda was called Pradosh Mitter.

'Yes, that's right,' Feluda acknowledged.

'There is a double room booked in your name on the ground floor,' the man replied.

We were handed the Visitors' Book to sign. Only a few lines above our own names, we saw two entries: Dr H.B. Hajra and Master M. Dhar.

The Circuit House was built on a simple plan. There was a large open space as one entered. To its left were the reception and the manager's room. In front of it was a staircase going up to the first floor, and on both sides, there were wide corridors along which stood rows of rooms. There were wicker chairs in the corridors.

A bearer came and picked up our luggage, and we followed him down the right-hand corridor to find room number 3. A middle-aged man, sporting an impressive moustache, was seated on one of the wicker chairs, chatting with a man in a Rajasthani cap. As we walked past them, the first man said, 'Are you Bengalis?' Feluda smiled and said, 'Yes.' We were then shown into our room.

It was quite spacious. There were twin beds, each with a mosquito net. Set apart, at one end, was a two-seater sofa, a pair of easy chairs, and a round table with an ashtray on it. There was also a dressing table, wardrobes and bedside tables. Lamps, glasses and flasks of water were placed upon the tables. The door to the attached bathroom was to the left.

Feluda asked the bearer to bring us some tea and switched the fan on. 'Did you see those two names?' he asked, sitting down on the sofa.

'Yes, but I hope that man with the thick moustache isn't Dr Hajra!' I replied.

'Why? What if he is? Why should it matter?'

I couldn't immediately think of a good reason. Feluda saw me hesitate and said, 'You didn't like the man, did you? You want Dr Hajra to be a pleasant, cheerful and friendly man. Right?'

Yes, Feluda was absolutely right. The man we just met appeared kind of crafty. Besides, he was probably quite tall and hefty. That was not how I would picture a doctor. The tea arrived just as Feluda finished a cigarette. The bearer placed the tray on the table and left. Someone knocked on our door almost at once. 'Come in!' said Feluda in a grand manner, sounding like an Englishman. The man with the moustache moved aside the curtain and came in.

'I am not disturbing you, am I?' he said.

'No, not at all. Please sit down. Would you like a cup of tea?'

'No, thanks. I've just had some. Frankly speaking, the tea here isn't all that good. But then, that's true of most places. India is the land of tea, yet how many hotels, or dak bungalows, or circuit houses serve good quality tea, tell me? But if you go abroad, it's a different story. Even in a place like Albania, I have had very good tea—would you believe it? First-class Darjeeling tea, it was. And if you went to Europe? Every major city would give you good tea. The only thing I don't like is the business of tea bags. Your cup is filled with hot water, and you're handed a little bag packed with tea leaves. A piece of string is tied to this bag. You have to hold it by this string and dip it in the water to make your own tea. Then you might add milk to it, or squeeze a lemon, as you wish. Personally, I prefer lemon tea. But you need really good tea for that. The kind of tea they have here is very ordinary.'

'You have travelled a lot, have you?' Feluda asked.

'Yes, that's all I've done in life,' our visitor replied. 'I am what you might call a globetrotter. And I'm fond of hunting. I got interested when I was in Africa. My name is Mandar Bose.'

I had heard of the globetrotter Umesh Bhattacharya, but not of Mandar Bose.

He probably guessed what I was thinking. 'I don't suppose my name will mean anything to you,' he said. 'When I first left home, my name appeared in the press. But that was thirty-six years ago. I've been back in India for only three months.'

'Really? I must say your Bengali has remained pretty good, considering you've been out of the country for so long.'

'Well, that's something entirely up to the person who's travelling abroad. If you want to forget your own language, you can do so in just three months. And if you don't, you'll not forget it even in thirty years. But I was lucky in that I came across other Bengalis frequently. When I was in Kenya, I ran a business trading in ivory. My partner there was a Bengali. We worked together for almost seven years.'

'Is there any other Bengali here in the Circuit House?' asked Feluda.

I had noticed earlier that he seldom wasted time on idle chit-chat.

'Yes! That's what I find so surprising. But one thing's become clear to me. People in

Calcutta are fed up. So they get out whenever they can. This man here, though, has come with a purpose. He's a psychologist. It's all a bit complicated. There's a little boy with him, about eight years old. He's supposed to be able to recall his previous life. Says he was born in some fort in Rajasthan, once upon a time. This man is roaming around everywhere with the boy, looking for that fort. What I can't tell is whether this psychologist is a fraud, or the boy is simply telling a pack of lies. His behaviour is certainly odd. He doesn't talk properly with anyone, doesn't answer questions. Very fishy. I've seen a lot of cheats and frauds all over the world— never thought I'd come across something like this back in my own country!'

'Was it your globetrotting that brought you here?'

Mr Bose smiled and stood up. 'To tell you the truth, I haven't yet seen much of this country...By the way, I didn't catch your names!'

Feluda made the introductions. 'And I have never stepped out of this country,' he added.

'I see. Well, if you come to the dining hall at around half past eight, we'll meet again. I believe in early-to-bed and early-to-rise, you see.'

We left our room with Mr Bose and emerged into the corridor outside. A taxi was coming in through the gate. It stopped under the portico, and a man of about forty got out of it, accompanied by a thin little boy. I did not have to be told that they were Dr Hemanga Hajra and Mukul Dhar.

FIVE

Mr Bose said 'good evening' to Dr Hajra as he passed him, and went towards his own room. Dr Hajra began walking down the corridor, holding the boy by the hand. Then he saw us and stopped, looking a little confused. Perhaps the sight of two strangers had startled him.

Feluda smiled and greeted him. 'Namaskar. Dr Hajra, I presume?' he asked.

'Yes. But I don't think I…?'

Feluda took out one of his cards from his pocket and handed it to Dr Hajra. 'I need to talk to you. To tell you the truth, we are here at Mr Dhar's request. He has written you a letter.'

'Oh, I see. Mukul, why don't you go to your room? I'll have a chat with these people, then I'll join you. All right?'

'I'll go to the garden,' said Mukul.

His voice sounded as sweet as a flute, but his tone was flat and lifeless, almost as if the words had been spoken by a robot. Dr Hajra said, 'Very well, you may go to the garden, but be a good boy and don't go out of the gate, okay?'

Mukul jumped from the corridor straight on to the gravel path, without saying another word. Then he stepped over a row of flowers and stood quietly on the lawn. Dr Hajra turned back to us, gave a somewhat embarrassed smile and asked, 'Where should we sit?'

'Let's go to our room.'

The hair around Dr Hajra's ears had started to grey, I noticed.

His eyes held a sharp, intelligent look. Now that I could see him more closely, he appeared older—probably in his late forties.

When we were seated, Feluda handed him Mr Dhar's letter and offered him a Charminar. Dr Hajra smiled, said, 'No, thanks', and began reading the letter. When he'd finished, he folded it and put it back in its envelope.

Feluda explained quickly about Neelu being kidnapped. 'Mr Dhar was afraid,' he said, 'that those men might have followed Mukul and arrived here. That is why he came to see me. In fact, I am here really because he wanted me to join you. But, even if nothing untoward happens and you do not require my protection, I can see that my visit will not go to waste as I've always wanted to see Rajasthan.'

Dr Hajra remained thoughtful for a few moments. Then he said, 'Fortunately, nothing has happened as yet that might be seen as untoward. But honestly, there was no need to talk to a press reporter and say so much. I told Mr Dhar to wait until I finished my investigation, and then he could get Mukul to speak to as many reporters as he liked, especially about the hidden treasure. I might think the story is possibly quite baseless, but there might well be people who'd be easily tempted to go and look for it!'

'What do you think of this whole business of recalling previous lives? Do you really believe in *jatismars*?'

'What I think amounts to shooting arrows in the dark or simply making guesses. Yet I cannot dismiss the idea as pure nonsense. After all, there have been similar cases in the past. What those people could recall turned out to be accurate, to the last detail. That is why, when I heard about Mukul, I decided to do a thorough investigation. If it turned out that everything Mukul could recall was true, then I would treat his case as a starting point and base my future research on it.'

'Have you made any progress?'

'One thing has become clear. I was right to think about Rajasthan and bring him here. Mukul's entire demeanour has changed from the moment we set foot in Rajasthan. Just think. For the first time in his life, he is away from his parents and others in his family and travelling with a virtual stranger. Yet he hasn't mentioned his own people even once in the last few days.'

'How is his relationship with you?'

'We've had no problems. He sees me as someone who's taking him to his dreamland. All he can think of is his golden fortress. So he jumps with joy each time he sees a fort.'

'Any sign of the golden fortress?'

Dr Hajra shook his head. 'No, I am afraid not. On our way here, I took him to the fort in Kisangarh. Yesterday evening, he saw the Jodhpur fort from outside. Today, we went to Barmer. Every time, he says, "No, not this one. Let's find another." One really needs patience in a case like this. I know there's no point in taking him to Chittor or Udaipur because there's no sand near those places. Mukul keeps talking of sand, and that's to be found only in these parts. So I'm thinking of going to Bikaner tomorrow.'

'Would you mind if we came along?'

'No, of course not. In fact, I'd feel quite reassured if you were with us because… something happened…'

Dr Hajra stopped. Feluda had taken out his packet of cigarettes, but did not open it.

'Yesterday evening,' Dr Hajra spoke slowly, 'there was a phone call.'

'Where?'

'Here in the Circuit House. I wasn't here; Mukul and I were out looking at the fort. In our absence, someone rang to ask if a man had arrived from Calcutta with a small boy. Naturally, the manager said yes.'

'But,' Feluda suggested, 'it could be that some of the locals know about the press report that appeared in Calcutta and simply wanted to verify it? After all, there are plenty of Bengalis in Jodhpur, aren't there? Surely a little curiosity in a matter like this is natural?'

'Yes, I can see that. But the question is, why didn't that man come here and meet me, or get in touch, even when he heard that I was here?'

'Hmm. Perhaps it's best that you and I stay together. And don't let Mukul go out on his own.'

'Are you mad? Of course I won't.' Dr Hajra rose. 'I have booked a taxi for tomorrow. As there are just two of you, we'll manage quite easily in one taxi.'

He began moving towards the door. Suddenly, Feluda asked a question rather unexpectedly: 'By the way, weren't you involved in a case in Chicago, about four years ago?'

Dr Hajra frowned. 'A case? Yes, I've been to Chicago, but…'

'Something to do with a spiritual healing centre?'

Dr Hajra burst out laughing. 'Ah, are you talking about Swami Bhavananda? The Americans used to call him Byavanyanda. Yes, there was a case, but what was reported in the press was grossly exaggerated. The man was certainly a cheat, but you'll find similar cheats among quacks of all kinds. It was small-time stuff, no more. In fact, his patients caught him out, and the news spread. Reporters from the press came to me for my opinion.

I said very little, and tried to play things down. But those reporters blew everything out of proportion. Afterwards, I happened to meet Bhavananda. I explained the whole matter to him myself and we parted as friends.'

'Thank you. What I read in the papers told me something quite different.'

We went out of the room together with Dr Hajra. It was dark outside. Although the western sky was still glowing red, the streetlights had come on. But where was Mukul? He was last seen in the garden, but now he wasn't there. Dr Hajra had a quick look in his room, and came out, looking concerned.

'Where's that boy gone?' he said and climbed down from the corridor on to the gravel path. We followed him. Mukul was certainly not in the garden.

'Mukul!' Dr Hajra called. 'Mukul!'

'Yes, he's heard you. He's coming!' said Feluda.

In the twilight, I could see Mukul coming back from the road outside and turn into the gate. At the same time, I saw a man on the opposite pavement, walking briskly towards the new palace on the eastern side. I did not see his face, but could see—even in the dark—that the colour of his shirt was bright red. Had Feluda seen him?

Mukul came towards us. Dr Hajra went to him, his arms outstretched, a smile on his lips. Then he said gently, 'You shouldn't go out like that!'

'Why not?' asked Mukul coldly.

'You don't know this place. There are so many bad people about.'

'I know him.'

'Who?'

Mukul pointed at the road. 'That man…who was here.'

Dr Hajra placed a hand on his shoulder and turned to Feluda. 'That's the trouble, you see,' he said. 'It's difficult to say whether he's talking of someone he really knows in this life, or whether he's still talking about his previous life.'

I noticed a shiny piece of paper in Mukul's hand. Feluda had seen it, too. He said, 'May I see that piece of paper you're holding?'

Mukul handed it to Feluda. It was a piece of golden foil, about two inches long and half an inch wide.

'Where did you find it?'

'Over there,' Mukul pointed at the grass.

'May I keep it?' asked Feluda.

'No. I found it.' Mukul's voice hadn't changed. His tone was just as cold and as flat. Feluda was obliged to return the piece of foil to him.

Dr Hajra said, 'Come on, Mukul, let's go to our room. We'll have a wash, and then we'll both go and have dinner. Goodnight, Mr Mitter. Early breakfast at half past seven tomorrow morning, and then we'll leave.'

Feluda wrote a postcard to Mr Dhar with news of Mukul's welfare before we went to the dining hall. By the time we got there after a shower, Dr Hajra and Mukul had returned to their room.

Mandar Bose was sitting in the opposite corner, having his pudding with the Marwari gentleman he had been talking to earlier. They finished their meal and rose as we were served our soup. Mr Bose raised his hand and said, 'Good night!' as he went out through the door.

After two nights on the train, I was feeling quite tired. All I wanted to do after dinner was go to sleep, but Feluda made me stay awake for a while. He took out his blue notebook and sat on the sofa. I was lying in my bed. We had a cream to ward off mosquitoes, so there was no need to use the mosquito net.

Feluda pushed the little button on his ballpoint pen, got it ready to write and said, 'Who have we met so far? Give me the whole list.'

'Starting from…?'

'Mr Dhar's arrival.'

'Okay, Sudhir Dhar. That's number one. Then Shivratan. Then Neelu. Oh, Shivratan's servant—'

'What was his name?'

'Can't remember.'

'Manohar. Next?'

'Jatayu.'

'What's his real name?'

'Lalmohan.'

'Surname?'

'Surname...his surname is...Ganguli!'

'Good.'

Feluda continued to write as I proceeded with my list. 'Then we saw that man in the red shirt.'

'Did we actually meet him? Get to know him?'

'No.'

'All right. Go on.'

'Mandar Bose, and that other gentleman.'

'And then we met Mukul Dhar. Doctor—'

'Feluda!'

My sudden scream made Feluda stop in mid-sentence. My eyes had fallen on Feluda's bed. An ugly, creepy creature was trying to slip out from under his pillow. I pointed at it. Feluda sprang to his feet, moved quickly and removed the pillow. A scorpion lay on the bed. Feluda pulled the bedsheet off in one swift motion and the scorpion fell on the ground. Then he grabbed his chappal and smacked it three times with all his might. After that, he tore off a piece from a newspaper, picked up the crushed creature with it and went into the bathroom. I saw him crumple the whole thing into a ball and throw it out of the back door.

He came back to the room and said, 'The door which the cleaners use was left open. That's how Mr Scorpion got into our room. Anyway, go to sleep now. We have an early start tomorrow.'

But I could not dismiss the matter so easily. Something told me...but I put the thought out of my mind. If I kept thinking of possible danger, and if my telepathy was strong enough, it might just drag that danger closer—who knew?

It would be far better to try to sleep.

SIX

The following morning, as soon as I emerged from our room, I heard a familiar voice say, 'Good morning!' It was Jatayu. Feluda was already seated on a chair on the corridor outside, waiting for his tea. Jatayu glanced round excitedly and said, 'Oh! This is such a thrilling place, Mr Mitter! Full of powerfully suspicious characters.'

'You are unharmed, I hope?' Feluda asked.

'Oh yes. I feel fitter than ever. This morning, you know what I did? I challenged the manager of our lodge to an arm-wrestle. But the fellow didn't accept.' Then he came a little closer and whispered,

'I have a weapon in my suitcase!'

'A catapult?'

'No, sir. A Nepali dagger, straight from Kathmandu. If I'm attacked, I'm going to stab my attacker with it—push it straight into his stomach, I tell you. Then let's see what happens. I've always wanted to build up a collection of weapons, you know.'

I wanted to laugh again, but my self-control was getting better, so I managed to stop myself. Lalmohan Babu sat down on the chair next to Feluda and asked, 'What's your plan today? Aren't you going to see the fort?'

'Yes, but not the fort in Jodhpur. We're going to Bikaner.'

'Bikaner? Why Bikaner?'

'We've got company. Somebody's arranged a car.'

Another voice said 'Good morning!' from a different part of the corridor. Mr Globetrotter was walking towards us. 'Did you sleep well?' he asked.

I caught Lalmohan Babu casting admiring glances at Mandar Bose's handsome moustache and muscular physique. Feluda introduced him to Mr Bose.

'Good heavens, a globetrotter!' Lalmohan Babu's eyes widened. 'I must cultivate you, dear sir. You must have had a lot of hair-raising experiences!'

'Plenty, I can assure you. The only thing that I have missed is being boiled in a cannibal's cooking pot. Apart from that, I have had virtually every experience a man can possibly have.'

Suddenly, I noticed Mukul. I hadn't seen him come out on the corridor. He was standing quietly in a corner, staring at the garden. Then Dr Hajra appeared, dressed and ready to go out. A flask was slung from one shoulder; from the other hung binoculars, and around his neck was the strap of his camera. He said, 'It will take us almost four and a half hours to get there. If you have a flask, take it with you. God knows if we'll get anything to drink on the way. But I've told the dining hall to give us four packed lunches.'

'Where are you off to?' asked Mandar Bose.

On being told where we were going, he became all excited. 'Why don't we all go together?' he asked.

'What a good idea!' exclaimed Lalmohan Babu.

Dr Hajra looked a little uncomfortable. 'Well then, how many are actually going?' he enquired.

'Look, there's no question of all of us going in one car,' Mr Bose reassured him. 'I will arrange another taxi. I think Mr Maheshwari would also like to go with me.'

'Are you going, too?' Dr Hajra asked Lalmohan Babu.

'If I go, I'll pay my share. I don't want anyone else to pay for me. Tell you what, why don't you four go in one taxi? I'll go with Mr Globetrotter.'

Obviously, Jatayu wanted to hear a few stories from Mr Bose and perhaps get ideas for a new plot. He had already written at least twenty-five adventure stories. To be honest, his remark made me feel quite relieved. Five in one car would have been cramped and uncomfortable.

Mr Bose spoke to the manager and booked a second taxi. Lalmohan Babu returned to New Bombay Lodge. 'Please pick me up on your way,' he said before he departed. 'I'll be ready in half an hour.'

Before I describe anything else about our visit to Bikaner, perhaps I ought to mention that Mukul rejected the fort there as soon as he saw it. But that was not the highlight of our visit. Something far more important happened in Devikund, which proved that we were truly up against a ferocious foe.

Nothing much happened on the way to Bikaner, except that we saw a group of gypsies.

They were camping by the roadside. Mukul asked us to stop, got out of the car and roamed amongst the gypsies for a while. Then he returned and declared that he knew those people.

After that, Feluda and Dr Hajra spoke about Mukul for a few minutes. I cannot tell whether he heard the conversation from the front seat. If he did, his demeanour gave nothing away.

'Dr Hajra,' Feluda began, 'when Mukul talks of his previous life, what exactly does he say?'

'He mentions one thing repeatedly—a golden fortress. His house was apparently near that fortress. Gold and jewels were buried under the ground in that house. From the way he talks, it seems as if he was present when the treasure was buried. Apart from that, he talks of a battle. He says he saw a large number of elephants, horses, soldiers, guns, cannons—there was a lot of noise, and people were screaming. And he talks of camels. Says he's ridden camels. Then he talks of peacocks. Once a peacock had attacked him, pecked his hand so hard that it began bleeding. There's something else he mentions frequently. Sand. Haven't you noticed how animated he becomes when he sees sand?'

We reached Bikaner at a quarter to twelve. The road began going uphill a little before we reached the city, which was surrounded by a wall, on top of the hill. The most striking building there was a huge fort, made of red sandstone.

Our car drove straight to the fort. As it got closer, the fort appeared to grow bigger. Baba was right. The appearance of the forts in Rajasthan was a good indicator of the might of the Rajputs.

As soon as our taxi drew up at the entrance, Mukul said, 'Why have we stopped here?'

Dr Hajra asked him, 'Does this fort seem familiar, Mukul?'

Mukul replied solemnly, 'No. This is a stupid fort, not the golden one.'

By this time, we had all climbed out of the car. Just as Mukul finished speaking, a harsh raucous sound reached our ears. At once, Mukul ran to Dr Hajra and flung his arms around him. The sound had come from a park opposite the fort.

'That was a peacock. Has this happened before?' asked Feluda.

Dr Hajra stroked Mukul's head gently. 'Yes. It happened yesterday in Jodhpur. He can't stand peacocks.'

Mukul had turned quite pale. 'I don't want to stay here,' he said, in the same lifeless yet sweet voice.

Dr Hajra turned to Feluda. 'I'm going to take the car and go to the local Circuit House. Then I'll send it back here. Why don't you two see whatever you want to? You can join me at the Circuit House when the car comes back to pick you up. But please make sure we leave here by two o'clock, or it will be late by the time we get back to Jodhpur.'

There was reason to feel disappointed, particularly for Dr Hajra, but I didn't mind all that much. I was about to step into a Rajasthani fort for the first time in my life. The thought was giving me goose pimples.

We proceeded towards the main gate of the fort. Suddenly, Feluda stopped and laid a hand on my shoulder. 'Did you see?'

'What?'

'That man.'

Was he referring to the man in the red shirt? I followed his gaze, but could not spot a single red shirt anywhere. There were lots of people milling about, for there was a small market just outside the fort. 'Where is he?' I asked.

'Idiot! Are you looking for a red shirt?'

'Yes. Shouldn't I? Who are you talking about?'

'You're the biggest fool on earth. All you remember is the shirt, nothing else. It was the same man, he was wearing a shawl and most of his face was covered, all except his eyes. But today he had a blue shirt on. When we stopped to look at those gypsies, I saw a taxi going towards Bikaner. That's when I spotted that blue shirt.'

'But what is he doing here?'

'If we knew that, there would be no mystery!'

The man had vanished. I passed through the gate and entered the fort, feeling rather agitated. A large courtyard greeted me. The fort stood proudly to the right. There were pigeons everywhere, in every niche in the wall. A thousand years ago, Bikaner was a thriving city, but it had disappeared under the sand. Feluda told me that four hundred years ago, Raja Rai Singh began building the fort. He was a famous leader in Akbar's army.

Something had been bothering me for a while. Why hadn't Lalmohan Babu and the others arrived yet? Did they get late in setting out? Or had their car broken down on the way? Then I told myself not to worry. There was no point in spoiling the joy of seeing an amazing historical sight.

What struck me as most amazing was the armoury. Not only did it contain weapons, but also a very beautiful silver throne, called Alam Ambali. It was said to be a gift from a Mughal badshah. Apart from that, there were swords, spears, daggers, shields, armour, helmets—there was no end to the weapons. The swords were so large and so strong that it seemed incredible that they were meant to be used by human beings. The sight of those weapons reminded me of Jatayu again. Funnily enough, as soon as I thought of him, he arrived, possibly dragged by the force of my telepathy. In that huge room in the massive fort, standing near a very large door, Jatayu looked smaller and more comical than ever.

When he saw us, he grinned, looked around and simply said, 'Was every Rajput a giant? Surely these things weren't made to be used by ordinary men?'

It turned out that my hunch was right. They had travelled for about seventy kilometres, when their taxi got a flat tyre. 'Where are the other two?' Feluda asked.

'They stopped to buy things in the market. I couldn't wait any longer, so I came in.'

We left the armoury and went off to see Phool Mahal, Gaj Mandir, Sheesh Mahal and Ganga Nivas. When we got to Chini Burj, we saw Mandar Bose and Mr Maheshwari. They were both clutching parcels wrapped with newspaper, so clearly they had done some shopping. Mr Bose said, 'The weapons I saw in the forts and castles in Europe—all built in medieval times—and the weapons I've seen here today, all prove one thing. The human race is becoming weaker every day, and smaller in size!'

'Like me, you mean?' Lalmohan Babu remarked with a smile.

'Right. Exactly like you,' Mr Bose replied. 'I don't think a single Rajput would have matched your dimensions in the sixteenth century. Oh, by the way,' he turned to Feluda, 'this was waiting for you at the reception desk in the Circuit House.'

He took out a sealed envelope from his pocket and passed it to Feluda. It had no stamp on it. Someone must have delivered it by hand. 'Who gave it to you?' Feluda asked, opening the envelope.

'Bagri, the fellow who sits at the reception desk. He handed it to me just as we were leaving. Said he had no idea who had dropped it off.'

'Excuse me,' said Feluda. Then he read the note, replaced it in the envelope and put it in his pocket. I could not tell what it said, nor could I ask.

We spent another half an hour in the fort. Then Feluda looked at his watch and said, 'Time to go to the Circuit House!' I didn't want to leave the fort, but knew I had to.

Both taxis were waiting outside. This time, we decided to leave together. As we were getting into ours, the driver told us that Dr Hajra and Mukul had not gone to the Circuit House. Apparently, Mukul had declared that he had no wish to go there. So where did they go? 'Devikund,' said the driver. Where was that? Not far from Bikaner, it turned out. Feluda said there were cenotaphs there (locally known as 'chhatris'), built as memorials to Rajput warriors.

We had to travel five miles, and it took us ten minutes. Devikund really was beautiful, as were the cenotaphs. Each cenotaph had stone columns that rose from stone platforms, supporting a small canopy, also made of stone. The whole structure, from top to bottom, was exquisitely carved. There were at least fifty such cenotaphs spread over the whole area. There were plenty of trees, all of them full of parrots. The birds were flocking together on some, or flitting from one tree to another, crying raucously. I had never seen so many parrots in one place.

But where was Dr Hajra? And Mukul?

Lalmohan Babu was getting restless. 'Very suspicious and mysterious!' he exclaimed.

'Dr Hajra!' shouted Mandar Bose. His deep, booming voice made a number of parrots take flight, but no one answered.

We began a search. There were so many cenotaphs that the place was like a maze. As we roamed amongst them, I saw Feluda pick up a matchbox from the grass and put it in his pocket.

In the end, it was Lalmohan Babu who found Dr Hajra. We heard him shout and ran to join him. Under a mango tree, in front of a mossy platform, Dr Hajra was lying crumpled on the ground. His mouth was gagged, and his hands were tied behind his back. He was groaning helplessly.

Feluda bent over him quickly, removed the gag and untied his hands. A torn piece

Under a mango tree, in front of a mossy platform, Dr Hajra was lying crumpled on the ground.

of a turban had been used to cover his mouth.

'How on earth did this happen?' asked Mr Bose.

Fortunately, Dr Hajra was not injured. He sat up on the grass and panted for a while. Then he told us what had happened. 'Mukul said he didn't want to go to the Circuit House,' he said, 'so we just drove on. Then we happened to come here. Mukul liked the place. "Those things are chhatris," he said. He had seen them before, and he wanted a closer look. So we got out of the car. Mukul began exploring, and I stood in the shade, under a tree. Suddenly someone attacked me from behind. He placed a hand over my mouth and knocked me down. I fell flat on my face. Then he pressed me down firmly—I think he kept his knee on the back of my head—and tied my hands, and then gagged my mouth.'

'Where's Mukul?' Feluda asked anxiously.

'I don't know. I did hear a car start soon after I was tied up.'

'You didn't see this man's face?'

Dr Hajra shook his head. 'No, but when we struggled, I got an idea of his clothes. He was wearing Rajasthani clothes, not a shirt and trousers.'

'There he is!' shouted Mandar Bose.

To my surprise, Mukul emerged from behind a chhatri, chewing a stalk of grass. Dr Hajra let out an audible sigh of relief. 'Thank God!' he cried.

'Where did you go, Mukul?'

No answer.

'Where were you all this while?'

'Behind that,' Mukul replied this time, pointing at a chhatri. 'I have seen such things before.'

Feluda spoke next. 'Did you see the man who was here?'

'Which man?'

Dr Hajra intervened, 'Mukul could not have seen him. He ran off to explore the area the minute he got out of the car. I never imagined such a thing would happen in Bikaner, so I wasn't unduly worried about him.'

Even so, Feluda tried again, 'Didn't you see the man who tied the doctor's hands?'

'I want to see the golden fortress,' said Mukul. It was clearly pointless to ask him anything else.

'Let's not waste our time any more,' Feluda spoke abruptly. 'In a way, I am glad that Mukul was nowhere near you. Or that man might have made off with Mukul. If he has returned to Jodhpur, we might be able to catch up with him, if we drive fast enough.'

In two minutes, we were all back in our cars and speeding back to Jodhpur. This time, Lalmohan Babu decided to join us. 'Those men drink a lot. I can't stand the smell of alcohol!' he confided.

Our Punjabi driver, Harmeet Singh, managed to drive at sixty mph. At one point, a small bird flew into our windscreen and died. Mukul and I were sitting in the front with the driver. I turned around once to look at the three men in the back seat. Lalmohan Babu was sitting crushed between Feluda and Dr Hajra. His face looked pale and his eyes were closed; nevertheless, a smile hovered on his lips, which told me that he could smell an adventure. Perhaps he had even thought of a plot for his next novel.

We drove at that speed for a hundred miles, but by that time it had become clear that the criminal had got away, and we wouldn't be able to catch up with him. After all, there was no reason to think that he wasn't travelling in a fast new car.

When we reached Jodhpur, it was dark and all the lights in the city had been switched on. Feluda said to Lalmohan Babu, 'You'd like to be dropped at the New Bombay Lodge, wouldn't you?'

'Yes,' Lalmohan Babu squeaked, 'I mean, all my things are there, so naturally…but I was wondering if…after dinner, I might go over to your place…?'

'Very well,' Feluda said reassuringly, 'I will ask at the Circuit House if they have a vacant room. You can ring me at around nine. I should be able to tell you then.'

I was still mulling over all that had happened during the day. We were up against someone extremely clever and crafty—of that there was no doubt. Was it the man in the red shirt, who went to Bikaner today wearing a blue one? I didn't know. Nothing was making any sense to me. Perhaps Feluda was just as puzzled. If he had worked things out, his whole demeanour would have changed. Having spent so many years with him and watched his reactions, that was something I had learnt to read quite well.

Upon reaching the Circuit House, we dispersed and went to our individual rooms. Before going to our room, Feluda said to Dr Hajra, 'If you don't mind, may I keep this with me?' In his hand was the torn piece of cloth with which Dr Hajra had been tied.

'Certainly,' Dr Hajra replied. Then he moved a little closer and lowered his voice. 'As you can see, Mr Mitter, the situation is now quite serious. This is exactly what you were afraid of, isn't it? I must say I hadn't anticipated such trouble.'

'Don't worry,' Feluda told him. 'You carry on with your work I am going to be with you. If you had gone straight to the Circuit House in Bikaner today, I don't think there would have been any problem. Fortunately, whoever attacked you could not kidnap Mukul. That's the main thing. From now on, stay close to us. That should minimize the chances of something similar happening again.'

Dr Hajra continued to look troubled. He said, 'I am not worried about myself, you see. If a scientist has to do research, he has to take certain risks just to complete his work. I am worried about you two. You are outsiders, not involved in this case at all.'

Feluda smiled. 'You must assume that I, too, am a scientist involved in some research, and so I'm taking risks as well!'

Mukul was pacing up and down the corridor. Dr Hajra called him, said 'Good night' to us and went to his room with Mukul. He was still looking preoccupied.

We went to ours. Feluda called a bearer and ordered two Coca-Colas. Then he took out his cigarettes and lighter from his pocket and placed them on the table. He was looking worried. From a different pocket, he took out the matchbox he had found in Devikund.

It had an ace printed on one side, and it was empty. Feluda stared at it for a few moments, before saying, 'We stopped at so many stations on the way to Jodhpur, and you saw so many paan stalls selling matches and cigarettes. Did you notice any of them selling this particular brand of matches?'

I had to admit the truth. 'No, Feluda, I didn't notice anything.'

'In western India, this brand with the ace on it is not sold anywhere—certainly not in Rajasthan. This matchbox has come from a different state.'

'Does that mean it doesn't belong to the man in the red shirt?'

'That is a foolish question. To start with, if a man is dressed as a Rajasthani, that doesn't automatically mean that he is one. Anyone can wear Rajasthani clothes. Secondly, plenty of other people could have gone to Devikund and attacked Dr Hajra.'

'Yes, of course. But we don't know who they are, do we? So what's the use of wondering about that?'

'See, you are speaking without thinking again. Lalmohan, Mandar Bose and Maheshwari—all three men reached the Bikaner fort quite late. Just think about that. Besides...'

'Oh. Yes, yes, now I can see what you mean!'

It just hadn't occurred to me before. Lalmohan Babu told us that their car had a flat tyre, which delayed them by forty-five minutes. What if he had lied? Even if he had told the truth and was quite innocent, Mandar Bose and Maheshwari could well have gone to Devikund instead of going to the local market.

Feluda let out a deep sigh and took out another object from his pocket. My heart gave a sudden lurch. I had totally forgotten about it. It was the letter Mandar Bose had handed him that morning.

'Who wrote that letter, Feluda?' I asked, my voice trembling.

'No idea,' Feluda replied, passing it to me. Only one line was written in large letters with a ballpoint pen:

If you value your life, go back to Calcutta immediately.

The note shook in my hand. I put it quickly on the table and placed my hands on my lap, trying to steady them.

'What are you going to do, Feluda?'

Feluda was staring at the ceiling fan. His eyes remained fixed on it as he muttered, almost to himself, 'A spider's web…geometry. It is dark now…so you can't see it…but when the sun rises, the web will catch its light…it will glitter…and then you can see its pattern. Now, all we have to do is wait for sunrise…!'

SEVEN

I woke for a few moments in the middle of the night—God knows what time it was—and saw Feluda scribbling something in his blue notebook, by the light of the bedside lamp. I don't know how long he stayed awake, but when I woke at half past six, he had showered, had a shave and was dressed to go out. According to him, when your brain works at high speed, you tend to sleep a lot less, but that does not affect your health. At least, that's what he believes. In the last ten years, I have not known him to be ill, even for a single day. Even here in Jodhpur, he was doing yoga every day. By the time I left my bed, he had finished his exercises.

When we went to the dining room for breakfast, we met everyone else. Lalmohan Babu had moved to the Circuit House the previous night. He had been given a room only two doors away Mandar Bose. We found him eating an omelette. He had thought of a wonderful plot, he told us. Dr Hajra still seemed upset. He had not slept well. Only Mukul seemed totally unperturbed.

Mandar Bose decided to be direct with Dr Hajra. 'Please don't mind my saying this,' he began, 'but you're dealing with such a weird subject that you're bound to invite trouble. In a country where superstition runs rife, isn't it better not to meddle with such things? One day, you'll find little boys in every household claiming to be *jatismars*! If you look closely, you'll find that their parents want a little publicity—that's all there is to it. But what are you going to do if that happens? How many kids will you take with you and travel all over the country?'

Dr Hajra made no comment. Lalmohan Babu simply cast puzzled glances from one to the other, for no one had told him about Mukul being able to recall his past life.

Feluda had already told me that after breakfast, he wanted to go to the main market. I knew he had some other motive; it could not be just to see more of the city, or to shop. We left at a quarter to eight, accompanied by Lalmohan Babu. I tried a couple of times to imagine him as a ferocious foe, but the mere idea was so laughable that I had to wipe it from my mind.

The area round the Circuit House was quiet, but the main city turned out to be noisy and congested. The old wall was visible from virtually every corner. Along that wall stood rows of shops, tongas, houses and much else. Remnants of a five-hundred-year-old city were now inextricably tangled with the modern Jodhpur.

We walked through the bazaar, looking at various shops. I could tell Feluda was looking for something specific, but had no idea what it was. Suddenly, Lalmohan Babu asked, 'What is Dr Hajra's subject? I mean, what is he a doctor of? This morning, Mr Trotter was saying something…?'

'Hajra is a parapsychologist,' Feluda replied.

'Parapsychologist?' Lalmohan Babu frowned, 'I didn't know you could add "para" before "psychologist"! I know you can do that to "typhoid". So does it mean it's half-psychology, just as paratyphoid is half-typhoid?'

'No, in this case "para" means "abnormal", not "half". Psychology is a complex subject, in any case. Parapsychology deals with its more obscure aspects.'

'I see. And what was all that about a *jatismar*?'

'Mukul is a *jatismar*. At least, that's what he's been called.'

Lalmohan Babu's jaw fell open.

'You'll get plenty of material for a plot,' Feluda continued. 'That young boy talks of a golden fortress he saw in a previous life. And the house where he lived had hidden treasure, buried under the ground.'

'Are we…are we going to look for those things?' Lalmohan Babu's voice grew hoarse.

'I don't know about you. We certainly are.'

Lalmohan Babu stopped, bang in the middle of the road, and grasped Feluda's hand with both his own. 'Mr Mitter! This is the chance of a lifetime! Please don't disappear anywhere without taking me with you. That's my only request.'

'But I don't know where we're going next. Nothing's decided.'

Lalmohan Babu paused for a while, deep in thought. Then he said, 'Will Mr Trotter go with you?'

'Why? Would you mind if he did?'

'That man is powerfully suspicious!'

There was a stall by the roadside, selling *naagras*. Most people in Rajasthan wear these shoes. Feluda stopped at the stall.

'Powerful he might be. Why suspicious?' he asked.

'When we were travelling to Bikaner yesterday, he was bragging a lot in the car. Said he had shot a wolf in Tanganyika. Yet I know that there are no wolves anywhere in Africa. I have read books by Martin Johnson. No one can fool me that easily!'

'So what did you say?'

'What could I say? I could hardly call him a liar to his face. I was sitting sandwiched between those two men. You've seen how broad his chest is, haven't you? At least forty-five inches. Both sides of the road were lined with huge cactus bushes and prickly pear. If I dared to contradict him, he'd have picked me up and thrown me behind one of those bushes—and then, in no time, I'd have turned into fodder for vultures. Great squadrons of vultures would have landed on me and had a feast!'

'You think so? How many vultures could possibly feed on your corpse?'

'Ha ha ha ha!'

Feluda had, in the mean time, taken off his sandals and put on a pair of *naagras*. He was walking back and forth in front of the stall.

'Very powerful shoes. Are you going to buy those?' Lalmohan Babu asked.

'Why don't you try on a pair yourself?' Feluda suggested.

None of the shoes were small enough to fit Lalmohan Babu, but he did slip his feet into the smallest pair that could be found, and gave a shudder. 'Oh my God! This was made from the hide of a rhino. You'd have to be a rhino yourself to wear such shoes.'

'In that case, you must assume that ninety per cent of Rajasthanis are rhinos.'

Both men took the *naagras* off and wore their own shoes again. Even the shopkeeper began laughing, having realized that the Babus from the city were having a little joke.

We left the stall and walked on. From a paan shop, a film song was being played very loudly on a radio. That reminded me of Durga Puja in Calcutta. Over here, people celebrated not Durga Puja, but Dussehra. But that was a long way away.

A few minutes later, Feluda suddenly stopped at a shop selling stoneware. It was a prosperous looking shop called Solanki Stores. Displayed in the showcase were beautiful

'Why don't you try on a pair yourself?' Feluda suggested.

pots, bowls, plates and glasses, all made of stone. Feluda was staring at those fixedly. The shopkeeper saw us, came to the door and invited us into his shop.

Feluda pointed at a bowl in the glass case, and said, 'May I see it, please?'

The shopkeeper did not pick up the bowl that was displayed. Instead, he took out an identical one from a cupboard. It was beautiful, made of yellow stone. I couldn't remember having seen anything like it before.

'Was this made here?' Feluda asked.

'It was made in Rajasthan, but not in Jodhpur.'

'No? Where was it made then?'

'Jaisalmer. This yellow stone can be found only in Jaisalmer.'

'I see.'

I had heard of Jaisalmer, but only vaguely. I didn't know where exactly in Rajasthan it was. Feluda bought the bowl. Then we took a tonga back to the Circuit House. It was half past nine by the time we returned, after a most bumpy ride. But it did mean that, after such a journey, our breakfast was certainly digested. Mandar Bose was sitting outside in the corridor, reading a newspaper. 'What did you buy?' he asked, looking at the packet in Feluda's hand.

'A bowl. After all, I must have a Rajasthani memento.'

'I saw your friend go out.'

'Who, Dr Hajra?'

'Yes. I saw him leave in a taxi, at around nine o'clock.'

'And Mukul?'

'He went with him. Perhaps they've gone to talk to the police. After what happened yesterday, Hajra must still be quite shaken.'

Lalmohan Babu returned to his room, on the grounds that he had to work on his new plot and change it a little. We went to ours.

'Why did you suddenly buy that bowl, Feluda?' I asked.

Feluda sat down on the sofa, unwrapped the bowl and placed it on the table, 'There is something special about it,' he said.

'What's so special?'

'Here is a bowl made of stone. Yet if I were to say it was a golden bowl, I wouldn't be far wrong! I have never seen anything like this in my life.'

After this, he lapsed into silence and began turning the pages of a railway timetable. There was little that I could do. I knew Feluda wouldn't open his mouth, at least for an hour. Even if I asked him questions, he wouldn't answer. So I left the room.

The corridor was now empty. Mandar Bose had gone. So had the European lady, who had been sitting at the far end earlier on. The sound of a drum reached my ears. Then someone started singing. I looked at the gate and found a boy and a girl, who looked like beggars. The boy was beating the drum and the girl was singing. They were walking towards the corridor. I went forward.

When I reached the open space, suddenly I felt like going upstairs. I had been walking past the staircase every day. I knew there was a terrace upstairs, but hadn't yet seen it. So I climbed up the steps.

There were four rooms upstairs. To the east and west of these was an open terrace. The rooms appeared to be unoccupied. Or it could be that the occupants had all gone out.

I went to the western side. The fort was clearly visible from here, looking quite majestic.

The two beggars downstairs were still singing. The tune of their song sounded familiar. Where had I heard it before? Suddenly I realized it was very similar to the tune I had heard Mukul hum at times. The same tune was being repeated every now and then, but it did not sound monotonous.

I went closer to the low wall that surrounded the terrace. It overlooked the rear portion of the Circuit House.

There was a garden at the back as well. I was considerably surprised to see it. All I had seen from one of the windows in our room was a single juniper tree standing at the back, but that gave no indication that there were so many trees spread over such a large area.

What was that bright blue object glittering behind a tree? Oh, it was a peacock. Most of its body was hidden behind the tree, so at first I couldn't see it properly. Now it emerged, and was pecking the ground. Was it looking for worms? As far as I knew, peacocks ate insects. Suddenly something I'd once read about peacocks came back to me. It is always difficult to find a peacock's nest. Apparently, they manage to choose the most inaccessible spots to lay their eggs and raise their young.

The peacock was moving forward, taking slow, measured steps, craning its neck and occasionally looking around. Its long tail followed the movement of its body.

Suddenly, the peacock stopped. It craned its neck to the right. What had it seen? Or had it heard something?

The peacock moved away. Something had disturbed it. It was a man, standing right below the spot where I was. I could see him through the gaps in the trees. The man had a turban on his head. It wasn't very large. He had wrapped a white shawl around himself. As I was standing above him, I could not see his face. All I could see were his turban and his shoulders. His arms were hidden under the shawl.

He began walking stealthily, moving from the western side of the building. I was on the terrace facing the west. Our room was on the ground floor, in the opposite direction.

I wanted to see where the man was going. So I ran past the rooms in the middle of the terrace, and leant over the wall on the eastern side.

The man was standing below me once again. If he looked up, he would see me. But he didn't. He was creeping closer to our room, to one of its windows. Then one of his hands slipped out from under the shawl. What was that, close to his wrist, glinting in the sun?

The man stopped. My throat felt dry. Then he took another step forward.

Suddenly, a loud, harsh sound broke the silence. The peacock had cried from somewhere. The man gave a violent start and, at the same moment, I screamed, 'Feluda!'

The man in the turban turned and ran in the same direction from which he had come. He disappeared in a matter of seconds. I sprinted down the stairs, taking two steps at a time, ran along the corridor without stopping, crashed straight into Feluda at the door to our room, and stood there, stunned.

Feluda pulled me inside and asked, 'What's the matter? What happened?'

'I saw from the roof a man . . . wearing a turban . . . walking towards your window!'

'What did he look like? Tall?'

'Don't know. Saw him from a height, you see. On his hand…was a…a….'

'A what?'

'Watch…!'

I thought Feluda would either laugh the whole thing off, or tease me by calling me an idiot and a coward. He did neither. Looking a little grim, he simply peered out of the window and looked around.

Someone knocked on our door.

'Come in!'

A bearer came in with coffee.

'Salaam, saab!' He placed the tray on the table and took out a folded piece of paper from his pocket. He handed it to Feluda, saying, 'Manager saab asked me to give it to you.'

He left. Feluda read the note quickly, then flopped down on the sofa, with an air of resignation.

'Whose letter is that, Feluda?'

'Read it.'

It was a short note from Dr Hajra, written on a sheet of paper that had his name printed in a corner. It said:

I believe it is no longer safe for me to remain in Jodhpur. I am going somewhere else, where I hope to have better success. I see no reason to drag you and your cousin into further danger. So I am leaving without saying goodbye. I wish you both all the very best.
Yours,
H.M. Hazra

'He has acted most hastily,' Feluda spoke through clenched teeth.

Then he made for the reception desk without even drinking his coffee.

Today, we found a different man at the desk. 'Did Dr Hajra say when he was going to be back?' Feluda asked.

'No, sir. He paid all his bills. Said nothing about coming back.'

'Do you know where he has gone?'

'To the railway station. That's all I know.'

Feluda thought for a moment. Then he said, 'It's possible to go to Jaisalmer by train from here, isn't it?'

'Yes, sir. We've had a direct line for two years.'

'When is the train?'

'It leaves at ten o'clock at night.'

'Is there a train in the morning?'

'Yes, but it goes only up to Pokhran. It should have left half an hour ago. One can go to Jaisalmer by this train, if one can arrange a car from Pokhran.'

'How far is it from Pokhran?'

'Seventy miles.'

'What other trains go from Jodhpur in the morning? I mean, to other destinations?'

The man consulted a book, leafing through a few pages. 'A train leaves for Barmer at eight o'clock. And at nine, there's the Rewari Passenger. That's all.'

Feluda's fingers beat an impatient tattoo on the counter. 'Jaisalmer is about 200 miles from here, isn't it?'

'Yes, sir.'

'Could you please arrange a taxi for us? We would like to leave for Jaisalmer at half past eleven.'

'Certainly, sir.' The receptionist picked up a telephone.

'Where are you off to?' asked a voice. It was Mandar Bose, coming out of his room with a suitcase in his hand. He had just had a shower and was smartly dressed.

'I'd like to see the Thar desert,' Feluda replied.

'Oh. So you're going to the northwest? I'm off to the east.'

'You are leaving Jodhpur, too?'

'My taxi should be here any minute. I don't like spending a very long time in any one place. Besides, if you leave as well, the Circuit House will become empty, in any case.'

The receptionist finished talking into the phone and turned to us. 'It's arranged,' he said.

'Topshe,' Feluda said to me, 'go and see if you can find Lalmohan Babu. Tell him we are going to Jaisalmer. If he wants to come with us, he should get ready immediately.'

I ran towards room number 10. It was not clear to me why we were suddenly going to Jaisalmer. Why did Feluda choose Jaisalmer, of all places? Was it because it was close to the desert?

Had Dr Hajra and Mukul also gone there? Did this mean that we were no longer in any danger? Or were we going to walk straight into it?

EIGHT

Pokhran was 120 miles from Jodhpur. Jaisalmer was another seventy. It should not take more than six or seven hours to cover 190 miles. Or, at least, that was what our driver, Gurbachan Singh, told us. He was a plump and cheerful Sikh. I saw him taking his hands off the steering wheel at times, and clasping them behind his head. Then he would lean back in his seat and take a little rest. But the car stayed on course because Gurbachan rested the steering wheel on his fat paunch, even moving it when necessary, without putting his hands back on it. This action was actually not as difficult as it may sound, for there was virtually no traffic on the road. Besides, the road ran straight, without curves or bends, for as much as five or six miles in many places. Unless something went wrong, we would reach Jaisalmer by six o'clock in the evening.

The scenery started to change when we were only ten miles out of Jodhpur. I had never seen anything like it. Jodhpur had a number of hills around it. The fort there was made of red sandstone that came from those hills. But now, those hills disappeared, and were replaced by an undulating terrain that stretched right up to the horizon. It was a mixture of grass, red earth, sand and loose stones. Ordinary trees and plants had disappeared, too. Now all I could see were acacia, cacti and similar plants whose names I didn't know.

The other thing I noticed was wild camels. They were roaming freely, like cattle and sheep. Some were light brown, like milky tea; others had darker coats, closer to black coffee. I saw one of them munching on a thorny plant. Feluda said that the thorns frequently injured a camel's mouth; but since those bushes were its only source of food, the camel put up with the discomfort.

Feluda also told me a little about Jaisalmer. It was built in the twelfth century, and became the capital of the Bhati Rajputs. Only sixty-four miles from there was the border between India and Pakistan. Even ten years ago, going to Jaisalmer was quite difficult. There were no trains, and what roads there were often disappeared under the sand. The place was so dry that if it rained just for a day in a whole year, people thought they were lucky. When I asked him about battles, Feluda said Alauddin Khilji had once attacked Jaisalmer.

We had travelled for nearly ninety kilometres (fifty-six miles), when purely out of the blue, we got a puncture, which made the car give an unpleasant shriek, lurch and come to a halt by the side of the road. I felt quite cross with Gurbachan Singh. He had assured us that he had checked the pressure in each tyre and all was well. As a matter of fact, the car appeared to be new and in good condition.

We got out with Gurbachan. It would take at least fifteen minutes to change the tyre. As soon as our eyes fell on the flat tyre, we realized what had caused the puncture. Strewn over a large area on the road were hundreds of nails. It was obvious that they were new and had been bought recently.

We exchanged glances. Gurbachan let out an expletive through clenched teeth that I shall not repeat here. Feluda said nothing. He simply stood there, arms akimbo, and stared at the road, deep in thought. His brows were drawn together in a frown. Lalmohan Babu took out a green notebook—it looked like a diary—from an old Japan Airlines bag, and scribbled something in it with a pencil.

By the time we finished changing the tyre, removed all the nails from the road and were ready to leave, it was a quarter to two.

Feluda said to Gurbachan, 'Sardarji, please keep an eye on the road. You can see that our enemies are trying to make things difficult for us!'

However, it wouldn't do to go too slowly, if we were to reach Jaisalmer before nightfall. So Gurbachan Singh reduced his speed from sixty to forty. If he were to keep his eye on the road all the time, he could hardly move faster than ten or fifteen miles an hour.

About forty miles later, when we had covered almost a hundred miles, the second disaster hit us. It simply could not be avoided. This time, instead of nails, thousands of drawing pins had been strewn over at least twenty feet of the road. Obviously, whoever wanted us to have a flat tyre was not taking any chances. What was also obvious was that Gurbachan Singh did not have another spare tyre.

We all climbed out again. If Gurbachan had not been wearing a turban, he would probably have scratched his head. Feluda asked him, 'Is Pokhran a town or a village?'

'It is a town, Babu.'

'How far is it?'

'About twenty-five miles.'

'Oh God. What are we going to do?'

Gurbachan tried to be reassuring. Every taxi that plied on that route, he said, was known to him. If we waited until another taxi came along, he would borrow a spare from its driver. Then we could go to Pokhran and have our own punctured tyres mended. The question was, would a taxi come along? If so, when? How long were we supposed to wait in the middle of nowhere?

A group of three men passed us by, leading five camels. They were going in the direction of Jodhpur. Each man had such dark skin that it looked almost black. One of them sported a snowy white beard and sideburns. I saw Lalmohan Babu move closer to Feluda, possibly because he had caught the men casting curious glances at us.

'Which is the nearest railway station from here?' Feluda asked, removing the pins from the road. We had all joined him in this good deed, to save other cars from a similar fate.

'Ramdeora. It is seven or eight miles from here.'

'Ramdeora...!'

When all the pins had been removed, Feluda took out a Bradshaw timetable from his shoulder bag. One particular page was folded. Feluda opened the timetable at that page, ran his eye over it and said, 'It's no use. The morning train that leaves Jodhpur reaches Ramdeora at 3.45. It must have left Ramdeora by now.'

'But isn't there another train to Jaisalmer at night?' I asked.

'Yes, but that will reach Ramdeora very early in the morning, at 3.53. If we began walking now, we'd take at least two hours to get to Ramdeora. There might have been a point in walking all that way, if there was any chance of catching the morning train. We could then have travelled to Pokhran, if nothing else. Now in this godforsaken . . .' Feluda broke off.

Even under such difficult circumstances, Lalmohan Babu smiled and said in a somewhat unsteady voice, 'Well, you must admit such a situation would be easier to find in a novel. Who knew even in real life...?'

Rather unexpectedly, Feluda raised a hand and stopped him. Our surroundings were completely silent, as if the entire world here had turned mute. In that silence, a faint noise reached our ears. There could be no mistake: chug-chug, chug-chug, chug-chug!

It was a train, the train to Pokhran. But where was the track?

I stared in the direction from which the noise was coming, and suddenly noticed a column of smoke. Almost immediately, I spotted a telegraph pole. I hadn't seen it before because the ground sloped down and the red pole practically merged with the reddish brown earth. Had it been standing on higher ground, outlined against the sky, it would have been far more easily visible.

'Run!' shouted Feluda and began running towards the smoke. I followed suit. Lalmohan Babu followed me. To my amazement, he ran so fast—despite his thin and scraggy appearance—that he nearly caught up with Feluda, leaving me behind.

I could see grass under my feet, but instead of being green, it was as white as cotton wool. We scrambled down the slope, still moving as fast as we could, and reached the railway track. The train was now within a hundred yards.

Without a second's hesitation, Feluda jumped into the middle of the track and began waving madly, both his arms raised high. The train began whistling loudly, but drowning the sound of the whistle rose Lalmohan Babu's voice: 'Stop! Stop! Halt, I say!'

Nothing worked. It was a small train, but not like the ones that Martin & Co. once used to run. If one stood by the tracks and raised a hand, those trains would stop, just like buses. This train, however, did nothing to reduce its speed. Whistling mightily, it came dangerously close, at which point Feluda was obliged to spring to safety. We simply stood and watched as the train coolly passed us by, clanging on its way, hiding the bright sun momentarily behind thick, black smoke. Even at a time like that, I couldn't help thinking that I might have seen such a scene only in a Hollywood western. Not once did I ever imagine I'd get to witness a scene like that in my own country!

'Such arrogance!' remarked Lalmohan Babu when the train had gone. 'It didn't look bigger than a caterpillar, did it?'

'Bad luck!' muttered Feluda, 'That train was running late, yet we couldn't take advantage of that. If we could have somehow got to Pokhran, we might have found another taxi.'

Gurbachan Singh, with great thoughtfulness, had collected our luggage and was carrying it over, but now there was no need for it.

I glanced briefly at the track. All that could be seen was smoke.

Suddenly, Lalmohan Babu spoke excitedly. 'What about camels?' he said.

'Camels?'

'Over there—look!'

Yes. Another group with camels was coming our way, this time from the direction of Jodhpur.

'Good idea, let's go!'

At Feluda's words, we began running again. 'When a camel really gets going, I've heard that it can cover twenty miles in an hour!'

Lalmohan Babu told me as he ran.

We managed to stop the group. This time, there were two men and seven camels.

'We need three camels, and we want to go to Ramdeora. How much would that be?' asked Feluda in Hindi. Then it turned out that the men spoke some local dialect. However, they could understand a little Hindi, and speak it, too, albeit haltingly.

Gurbachan spoke on our behalf. In the end, they agreed to lend us their camels for ten rupees.

'Can your camels run fast?' Lalmohan Babu wanted to know,

'We have a train to catch!'

Feluda laughed. 'Don't worry about running. Get on the camel first.'

'Get on…on its back?'

Perhaps for the first time, face to face with a camel, Lalmohan Babu realized the complexities involved in climbing on to its back. I was looking carefully at the animals. They looked perfectly weird, but had been saddled with care. On their backs were the kind of sheets with fringes and tassels that I'd seen earlier on elephants. On top of this sheet was a wooden seat. The sheet was covered with red, blue, yellow and green geometric patterns. Each camel had its long neck wrapped with a length of red fabric decorated with cowrie shells. It was clear that, in spite of their strange appearance, their owners loved and cared for them.

Three camels were now kneeling on the ground. Gurbachan Singh, by this time, had fetched every piece of our luggage, which consisted of two suitcases, two holdalls and a

Without a second's hesitation, Feluda jumped into the middle of the track and began waving madly,

both his arms raised high. The train began whistling loudly…

few smaller items. Gurbachan told us to wait for him in Pokhran, if we could catch the train in Ramdeora. He would definitely get to Pokhran that night. Our luggage was tied securely on to two of the other camels.

The first three camels were still waiting for us.

'You saw how they sat down, didn't you?' Feluda asked Lalmohan Babu. 'A camel folds its forelegs first, and the front part of its body comes down before its rear. When it gets up, expect just the opposite. It will raise its hind legs first. If you can remember that and lean backwards and forwards accordingly, you can avoid a great deal of embarrassment.'

'Emb-embarrassment?' Lalmohan Babu croaked.

'Here, watch me!'

Feluda jumped on to the back of the first camel. One of the men made a funny noise through his teeth. At once, the camel raised itself—quickly but awkwardly—in exactly the same manner that Feluda had just described. But he managed very well, there was no awkwardness.

'Come on, Topshe! You two are smaller and lighter than me, it should be easier for you,' Feluda called.

Both the Rajasthani men were grinning at our antics. I gathered all my courage and got on the second camel, which stood up immediately. Now I could tell where the real problem lay. When the hind legs were raised, the rider on the camel's back was likely to slide forward in one swift motion. If one could lean back and remain in that position as the camel rose to its feet, it would be easier to maintain one's balance. If I ever had to ride a camel again, I must remember that, I told myself.

'Dear G-ya-aa-d!' said Lalmohan Babu.

'God' became 'Gyad' for the simple reason that, even as he was uttering those words, the rear portion of the camel's body jerked into motion and Lalmohan Babu slid forward on its back. In the next instant, he was thrown back in the opposite direction. I heard him gulp noisily, as he lay horizontal on the camel's back, cast into an undignified heap.

Having said goodbye to Gurbachan Singh, we three Bedouins began our journey to Ramdeora.

'We must get to Ramdeora in half an hour. It's eight miles from here, isn't it? We have a train to catch!' Feluda yelled to the two men. At these words, one of them jumped up on his camel and marched forward briskly to take the lead. The second man shouted, 'Hei! Hei!' and every camel broke into a run.

As it was, the animals were ungainly and not exactly easy to sit on. When they lurched forward, my whole body swung and shook from side to side; but I didn't mind. We were running across a sandy terrain, covered with dry, scorched grass, and the place was Rajasthan—so, all in all, it was a thrilling experience.

Feluda was ahead of me, and Lalmohan Babu's camel was behind me. Feluda turned his head and called out, 'How do you find the ship of the desert, Mr Ganguli?'

I, too, looked back to see what Lalmohan Babu was doing. I found him making an awful grimace, as if he was in a freezing cold climate. His lips had parted, his teeth were clenched, and the veins on his neck were all standing out.

'What's the matter?' Feluda went on. 'Why don't you say something?'

Six words emerged from Lalmohan Babu, in five instalments: 'Ship...all right...but... talking...impossible!'

Laughter began bubbling up inside me once again, but I quelled it and focussed on the journey. We were now running alongside the railway track. In the distance, a column of smoke seemed to rise for a minute; then it disappeared. The sun was going down in the western horizon, and the landscape was changing. A hazy range of hills was visible in the far distance. On our right was a huge sand dune, unmarked by human feet. It was covered with wavy lines from top to bottom.

Perhaps the camels were not used to running fast for any length of time, so their speed faltered every now and then. When that happened, one of the men barked, 'Hei! Hei!' again, and the animals ran faster.

Around a quarter past four, a square structure came into view. It appeared to be a building, right next to the railway track. What could it be, if it wasn't a railway station?

As we got closer, it became clear that we were right. There was a signal, too. So it had to be a station, and the place had to be Ramdeora.

The camels had slowed down again. But now there was no need to shout at them. The train we were hoping to catch had come and gone. We couldn't tell when it had left, but there could be no doubt that we had missed it.

It meant only one thing. Until three o'clock in the morning, we would have to wait in this unknown place, in the middle of nowhere, by the side of the tiny structure that was trying to pass itself off as a station. And there was not a soul in sight.

NINE

It turned out that the station was in the process of being built. All it had at the moment was a platform and that structure, which was really a ticket window. Heaven knew when the building work would be completed. We selected a spot close to the ticket window and sat on our holdalls, preparing ourselves for a long wait. A kerosene lamp hung from a wooden post nearby, so when it got dark, we would at least be able to see one another.

There appeared to be signs of habitation not all that far from the station. Feluda went to have a look, then returned and said that although he had seen houses, there were no shops and nowhere to eat. All we had with us was a little water in our flasks, and Lalmohan Babu had a tin of *goja* (deep-fried pastry dipped in syrup). Perhaps we would have to spend the whole night on the strength of those.

The sun had set about ten minutes ago. It would soon be dark. Gurbachan Singh's arrival did not seem likely, as in the last three hours, we had not seen a single car go past, either towards Jodhpur or Jaisalmer. There was nothing to do but wait on the platform until the next train came at three o'clock.

Feluda was sitting on his suitcase and gazing steadily at the track. I watched him cracking the fingers of his right hand with his left. Obviously, he was anxious or agitated about something, which was why he wasn't saying much.

Lalmohan Babu opened his tin, bit into a *goja* and said, 'Who knew this would happen? If I didn't travel with you in the same compartment on the way from Agra, the entire nature of my holiday would not have changed like this, would it?'

'Why, do you mind?' Feluda asked.

'No, of course not!' Lalmohan Babu laughed. 'But it would certainly help if a few things were a bit clearer.'

'Which things in particular?'

'I don't really know what's going on, do I? I feel a bit like a shuttlecock—slapped from one side to the other, and back again. I mean, I don't even know who you are. Are you the hero, or the villain? Ha ha!'

'Why do you want to know? What would you do, anyway, if you knew?' Feluda asked with a smile. 'When you write a novel, do you reveal everything at the outset? Why don't you treat this entire Rajasthani experience as a novel? When it comes to an end, every mystery will be cleared up.'

'And I? Will I still be alive, and in one piece?'

'Well, you've already proved that you can run faster than a rabbit, if you have to. Isn't that reassuring enough?'

I hadn't realized it before, but someone had come and lit the kerosene lamp while we were talking. In its light, I suddenly saw two men, clad in local Rajasthani garb with turbans on their heads, making their way towards us. In their hands were stout sticks, which they were tapping on the ground. They stopped a few feet away, squatted and began a conversation in a completely incomprehensible language.

One thing about those men made my jaw fall open. Both were sporting huge moustaches. They didn't just turn upward, but had, in fact, coiled at least four times on either side of the men's faces. The final effect was like the spring fitted inside a clock. If they were pulled straight, each side would probably measure eighteen inches. Lalmohan Babu, too, seemed totally dumbstruck by the sight.

'Bandits!' muttered Feluda under his breath.

'Really?' Lalmohan Babu quickly poured himself some water from the flask and gulped it down.

'Undoubtedly.'

Lalmohan Babu tried to replace the lid on his tin, but dropped it on the platform with a loud clang. The noise made him jump, and he became more nervous.

I looked at the two men closely. Their skin was as dark and shiny as a freshly polished shoe. One of them took out a cigarette, placed it between his lips, and slapped all his pockets until he found a matchbox in one of them. But it turned out to be empty, so he threw it away on the track.

A sudden noise made me glance at Feluda. He had flicked his lighter on and was offering it to the man. The man looked taken aback at first, then leant forward to light his cigarette. After that, he took the lighter from Feluda and examined it closely, pressing it here and there before finding the right spot and lighting it once more. Lalmohan Babu tried to speak, but his voice sounded choked.

The man switched the lighter on and off a few times, before returning it to Feluda. Lalmohan Babu began stuffing his tin back into his suitcase, but it slipped from his hand and, this time, the whole tin fell on the ground, making a racket that was ten times worse than the previous one. Feluda paid him no attention. He simply took out his blue notebook from his shoulder bag and began leafing through its pages in the dim light from the kerosene lamp.

Suddenly, my eyes fell on a thorny bush a little way beyond the ticket window. A light was falling on it. Where was it coming from?

It was growing brighter. Then I heard a car. It was coming from the direction of Jaisalmer. Oh good. Perhaps Gurbachan Singh would now be able to borrow a spare tyre.

The car came into view, then whooshed past the little station and vanished towards Jodhpur. My watch showed half past seven.

Feluda raised his eyes from his notebook and looked at Lalmohan Babu. 'Lalmohan Babu,' he said, 'you write novels, don't you? You must know a lot of things. Can you tell me what a blister is, and what causes it?'

'Blister? . . . Blister?' Lalmohan Babu sounded completely taken aback. 'Why does one get blisters, you mean? But one could, quite easily. I mean, suppose you burnt your finger while lighting your cigarette...'

'Yes. But why should that cause a blister?'

'Oh. I see. Why? You want to know the reason?'

'All right, never mind. Tell me something else. If you look at a man from a height, why does he appear short?'

Lalmohan Babu simply stared without a word. Even in that dim light, I could see him rubbing his hands uncertainly. The two Rajasthani men were still talking in that same language, using the same tone. Feluda's eyes were fixed on Lalmohan Babu's face.

Lalmohan Babu licked his lips and found his voice. 'Why are you...I mean, all these questions...?'

'I have one more. And I'm sure you know the answer to this one.'

Lalmohan Babu said nothing. It was as if Feluda had hypnotized him.

'This morning, what were you doing among the trees behind the Circuit House, creeping up to my window?'

Just for a moment, Lalmohan Babu remained motionless. Then life returned to his limbs, and he burst into speech. 'But I was going to see you!' he declared, gesticulating wildly. 'Believe me, Mr Mitter, it was you I wanted to see. But that peacock made such a racket, and then I heard someone scream...so I got all startled and nervous and so...!'

'Was that the only way to get to my room? And was it necessary to wear a turban and a shawl to come and see me?'

'Look, that shawl was only a bed sheet. I took it from my room. And the turban? That was a towel from the Circuit House. I had to have some sort of a disguise, don't you see? Or how could I spy on that man?'

'Which man?'

'Mr Trotter. Very suspicious, that man. But thank goodness I did go there. See what I found, lying on the grass outside his window. It's a secret code. I was going to pass it on to you, when that peacock cried out and spoilt everything!'

I was looking carefully at Lalmohan Babu's watch. Yes, it was the same watch I had seen from the terrace in the Circuit House.

Lalmohan Babu opened his suitcase and groped in it. He fished out a crumpled piece of paper and handed it to Feluda. I could see that it had been screwed into a ball, but straightened later.

I peered over Feluda's shoulder to see what was written on it with a pencil. It said:

IP 1625+U

U – M

Feluda frowned darkly at the piece of paper. Was it algebra? I couldn't make head or tail of it. Lalmohan Babu whispered a couple of times, 'Highly suspicious!'

Feluda was muttering to himself, 1625...1625...where have I seen that number recently?'

'Could it be the number of a taxi?' I asked.

'No. 1625...sixteen twenty-fi—!' Feluda left his sentence incomplete and pounced upon his shoulder bag. Then he took out the railway timetable and opened it at the page that was folded. He ran a finger quickly down the page, and stopped abruptly.

'Yes, here it is. 1625 is the arrival.'

'Where?'

'Pokhran.'

'In that case,' I remarked, 'the "P" might mean "Pokhran". 1625 in Pokhran. What about the rest?'

'The rest is..."IP" and then "+U"...what could it...?'

'I don't like that "M" in the second line,' Lalmohan Babu told us.

'The letter M always reminds me of the word "murder".'

'Wait, dear sir, let me first deal with the top line!'

Lalmohan Babu continued to mutter under his breath, 'Murder...mystery... massacre...monster...!'

Feluda sat with the piece of paper on his lap, lost in thought.

Lalmohan Babu took out his tin of goja and offered it to me again.

When I'd taken one, he turned to Feluda and said, 'By the way, how did you know I'd crept up to your window? Did you see me?'

Feluda helped himself to a goja. 'You took your turban off, but did not brush your hair. When I met you shortly after the incident, the state of your hair made me quite suspicious.'

Lalmohan Babu smiled. 'I hope you won't mind my saying it, sir, but you strike me as a detective. A hundred per cent, full-fledged detective!'

Without saying anything, Feluda handed him one of his cards.

Lalmohan Babu's eyes began glinting.

'Oh. Pradosh C. Mitter! Is that your real name?'

'Yes. Why, is there something wrong with it?'

'No, no. But isn't it strange?'

'What is?'

'Your name. Look, it matches your profession. P-r-a-d-o-s-h, pronounced pro-dosh. "Pro" stands for "professional"; and "dosh" is the Bengali word for "crime". The "C" is "to see", that is "to investigate". So the whole thing works out as Pradosh C = Professional

Crime Investigator!'

'Great. Well done. But what about "Mitter"?'

'Mitter? Oh, that . . . I'll have to think about it,' said Lalmohan Babu, scratching his head.

'There's no need. I can solve it for you. You have seen meters on taxis, haven't you? It's the same thing—that is to say, it's an indicator.

So it doesn't just investigate, it also indicates. It picks out the criminal after an investigation and points a finger at him. Would you go along with that?'

'Bravo!' said Lalmohan Babu, clapping. But Feluda grew serious again. He glanced at the code, transferred it to his shirt pocket and took out a cigarette.

'The "I" and the "U" can be easily explained,' he said, 'that "I" is probably the fellow who wrote the code. And "U" is "you". But that plus sign doesn't make sense. And the second line is totally obscure...Look, Topshe, why don't you spread your holdall on the platform here and try to get some sleep? You, too, Lalmohan Babu. The train won't be here for another seven and a half hours. I will wake you up at the right time.'

It was not a bad idea. I unstrapped our holdall and spread it out.

As soon as I lay flat on my back, my eyes went to the sky and I realized I had never seen so many stars in my life. Was the sky so clear because we were close to a desert? Perhaps.

Soon, my eyes grew heavy with sleep. Once, I heard Lalmohan Babu say, 'I say, riding a camel has made my joints ache!' Then I thought I heard him mutter, 'M is murder.' After that I fell asleep.

The next thing I knew, Feluda was trying to shake me awake. 'Topshe! Get up, here comes the train!'

I scrambled to my feet and began rolling my holdall. By the time the straps had been fastened, the headlight on the train had come into view.

The various drafts of title calligraphy done by Ray

[illegible]

Pradosh C Mitter (Nicknamed Felu) – 35

Felu is a first-rate private investigator whose interest ranges far beyond crime. He is not without a streak of vanity, but that usually shows in the presence of his young cousin Tapesh or his writer-friend Lalmohan Ganguly. He has a keen understanding of human beings, both physical and moral courage & he has a wit which can turn into sarcasm — especially when he is dealing with his friend writer. As a private detective, Felu's earnings are reasonable, but he still doesn't own a car. As for Felu's views on the other sex, these are not known since no female characters appear [illegible]

Lalmohan Ganguly – 40

Lalmohan is a best-selling writer of cheap, popular thrillers. He is a great admirer of Felu, & ever since getting to know him, he has improved as a writer thanks to Felu's advice & criticism. Lalmohan loves adventure, though he is far from being a daredevil type himself. In fact, his courage derives from the fact that he has Felu as an ally. His zest for life is enormous, though as a [illegible] he falls far short of his friend. He is much wealthier than Felu, & owns a car.

Ray introduced the character of Jatayu aka Lalmohan Ganguly in *Sonar Kella*. The blueprint of the trio (Feluda, Topse and Jatayu) as he visualized them is noted down in detail in his literary notebook. It is to be noted that the illustration of Jatayu in the book is very different from the character played by Santosh Dutta in the film.

Topshe (18) the cousin of Feluda.

Topshe is the Watson & the chronicler of Feluda Holmes' adventures. Topshe hero-worships Feluda & believes he (Feluda) can do no wrong. Occasionally, Topshe has to use his own wits & does it with credit. Feluda also tries to develop Topshe's deduction powers by posing him questions, & discussing a case partly with him. Topshe also respects Feluda's moods & his silences.

We are very fortunate in being able to show a package of Dutch films in Calcutta, & for this we thank the Netherlands Govt. Holland has been making films from the very beginning of the century, but our familiarity with Dutch cinema is virtually nil. We know of two great Dutch makers of documentaries – Joris Ivens and Bert Haanstra, & we have been lucky enough to see some of their films. But that is where our familiarity ends. The present festival will, we hope, give us some idea of what is happening in Dutch cinema today.

I have great pleasure in declaring this festival open.

This is an opportunity when we are ... to see films from other European countries

Another page where Ray has written about the description of the trio. It is very interesting that although Ray wrote *Sonar Kella* in Bengali, he made notes on the character sketches in English.

সোনার কেল্লা

সত্যজিৎ রায়

36 pt.

||১|| — 14 ...

ফেলুদা খবরের কাগজটা সশব্দে ভাঁজ করে টেবিলের উপর ছুঁড়ে ফেলে একটা [illegible] হাই তুলে বলল, 'প্যারাসাইকলজি।'

আমি জিজ্ঞেস করলাম, 'হঠাৎ কি প্যারাসাইকলজির কথা ভাবছিলে তুমি?'

[illegible]

[illegible]

[illegible]

RS/SS131

The first page of the draft of *Sonar Kella* from the literary notebook

সোনার কেল্লা

P/C

PRE-CREDITS SEQ

কলকাতা। শীত কাল। মধ্যরাত্রি।

উত্তর কলকাতার একটা নিস্তব্ধ রাস্তা। রাস্তার ধারে কাপড়ঢাকা রিক্সা
দাঁড় করানো রয়েছে। রিক্সাওয়ালারা কম্বল মুড়ি দিয়ে ঘুমোচ্ছে।
একটা বেড়াল একটা কাঁচওয়ালা পাঁচিলের উপর দিয়ে হেঁটে গেল।
কোথায় যেন কুকুর ডাকছে।

একটা মধ্যবিত্ত ঘরের বাড়ির দোতলার ঘর। খাটের উপর মশারি
খাটানো। তার ভিতরে একটি বছর তিরিশের ভদ্রমহিলা ঘুমোচ্ছেন।
তার পাশে একটি বছর তিনেকের মেয়ে। সেও ঘুমোচ্ছে।
এবার ক্যামেরা প্যান করে মশারির পাশে একটি খালি বালিশের উপর
থামে। যে শুয়েছিল, উঠে গেছে।

ক্যামেরা বালিশ থেকে ঘুরে দেয়ালের উপর প্যান করে একটা
খোলা দরজার উপর থামে। দরজা দিয়ে পাশের ঘরে একটা
টেবিলের সামনে একটি ছেলেকে উবুড় হয়ে বসে মনোযোগ
দিয়ে খাতার কাগজে কী আঁকি করতে দেখা যায়।

ক্যামেরা zoom করে এগিয়ে যায়। ছেলেটি ছবি আঁকছে।

ছেলেটির মা-র (মালতী) ঘুম ভেঙে যায়। বালিশ খালি দেখেই উঠে
বসে। পাশের ঘরের দিকে দেখে; তারপর বিছানা ছেড়ে উঠে আসে।
তাদের ঘরে অন্যখাটে ছেলেটির বাবা (সুধীর) ঘুমোচ্ছে। মালতী
ঠেলে তাকে তুলে দেয়।

মালতী উগ্র - স্বরে —

সুধীর চোখ খুলেই টেবিলের দিকে দেখে। ছেলেটির ভ্রূক্ষেপ নেই,
সে একমনে এঁকে চলেছে। সুধীর খাটের উপর উঠে বসে।
মালতী টেবিলের এক পাশে গিয়ে দাঁড়ায়। ও কী আঁকে দেখে।

মালতী ও কী অবস্থা হল তোর? মুকুল!

সুধীর খাটের থেকে এসে মালতীর কাঁধে হাত রাখে।

মালতী চোখে ঘুম নেই - মুখে হাসি নেই!

The first page of the draft of the film *Sonar Kella* from the *kheror khata*

Ray jots down the first idea of a Feluda adventure set in Rajasthan in his literary notebook

LEFT TO RIGHT: The cover of the first edition of *Sonar Kella* designed by Ray (published in 1971 by Ananda Publishers) was changed after the film was released in 1974. The new cover featured an iconic still from the climax of the film.

Far Left: The cover of the French edition of the book

Near Left: The cover of the Japanese version of the book

The covers of the Italian and Malayalam translations of *Sonar Kella*

A 30' x 40' poster of *Sonar Kella*

Another poster of the film designed by Ray featuring the scorpion

LEFT: The cover of the Bengali film booklet
ABOVE: The cover of the English film booklet

LEFT: The insignia done by Ray in the booklet accompanying the summary of the film
RIGHT: The inside pages of the booklet

পশ্চিমবঙ্গ সরকারের তথ্য ও জনসংযোগ বিভাগ কর্তৃক প্রযোজিত

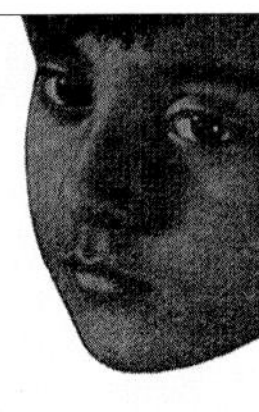

কাহিনী, সংগীত, চিত্রনাট্য ও পরিচালনা / সত্যজিৎ রায়

পরিবেশনা / ছায়াবাণী প্রাইভেট লিমিটেড

ক্যামেরা
সৌমেন্দু রায়
সম্পাদনা
দুলাল দত্ত
শিল্পনির্দেশক
অশোক বোস
মেক-আপ
অনন্ত দাশ
কর্মসচিব
অনিল চৌধুরী
ব্যবস্থাপনা
ভানু ঘোষ
ড্রেসার
হারু দাশ
শব্দগ্রহণ (স্টুডিও)
জে. ডি. ইরাণী
শব্দগ্রহণ (আউটডোর)
অনিল তালুকদার
অর্ন্তদৃশ্যগ্রহণ
ইন্দ্রপুরী স্টুডিও
ল্যাবরেটরি
ইউনাইটেড সিনে ল্যাবরেটরি
ইস্টম্যানকালার
জেমিনি কালার ল্যাবরেটরি
মাদ্রাজ
রিরেকর্ডিং
মঙ্গেশ দেশাই
রাজকমল কলামন্দির, বোম্বাই
আবহ-সঙ্গীত রেকর্ডিং
সমীর মজুমদার
স্থিরচিত্র
নিমাই ঘোষ
সন্দীপ রায়
টেকনিকা

হিন্দীসংলাপ
হৃদয়েশ পাণ্ডে
গান
সোহিনী দেবী (বিকানীর)
রমজান অম্মু
সিদ্দিকি

সহকারীবৃন্দ
পরিচালক
রমেশ সেন
শান্তিকুমার চট্টোপাধ্যায়
সুভাষ দে
সংগীত
অলোকনাথ দে
ক্যামেরা
পূর্ণেন্দু বোস
অনিল ঘোষ
কানাই দাশ
সম্পাদনা
কাশীনাথ দাশ
শিল্পনির্দেশক
সুরথ দাশ
মেক-আপ
কৃষ্ণ ঘোষ। সমীর গাঙ্গুলী
ব্যবস্থাপনা
বলাই আঢ্য
ত্রৈলোক্য দাশ
শৈবাল গুপ্ত
শব্দগ্রহণ (স্টুডিও)
সিদ্ধিনাথ নাগ। মাণিক
শব্দগ্রহণ (আউটডোর)
নিতাই জানা
প্রচার ও প্রচার অংকণ
বিদ্যুৎ চক্রবর্তী

৬ বছরের ছেলে মুকুলের ধারণা হয়েছে তার শৈশব কেটেছিল
সোনার কেল্লার দেশে।
সেখানে নাকি সে উট দেখেছে, ময়ূর দেখেছে,
বালির উপর যুদ্ধ দেখেছে।
ডাঃ হেমাঙ্গ হাজরা জন্মান্তর নিয়ে গবেষণা করছেন।
তিনি মুকুলকে পরীক্ষা করে সন্দেহ করেন যে
সে হয়ত পশ্চিম রাজস্থানে তার পূর্বজন্মের কথা বলেছে।
মুকুলকে সঙ্গে নিয়ে তিনি যোধপুর যাওয়া স্থির করেন।
সেখান থেকে শুরু হবে সোনার কেল্লা অনুসন্ধান।

যাবার আগের দিন মুকুল একটি সাংবাদিককে বলে
সে নাকি তার পূর্বজন্মের ছেলেবেলায়
তার বাড়ীতে অনেক দামী মণিমুক্তা দেখেছে।
সাংবাদিকের ধারণা হয় মুকুল গুপ্তধনের কথা বলছে, এবং
সেইভাবেই খবরটি পরদিন কাগজে ছাপা হয়।

দুই দুবৃত্ত—মন্দার বোস ও অমিয়নাথ বর্মন—খবরটা প'ড়ে
গুপ্তধনের লোভে যোধপুর রওনা দেয়।

ইতিমধ্যে, ছেলের বিপদের আশঙ্কা ক'রে মুকুলের বাবা সুধীর ধর
শখের ডিটেকটিভ ফেলু মিত্তিরের শরণাপন্ন হন। ফেলু তার খুড়তুতো
ভাইকে সঙ্গে নিয়ে যোধপুরের উদ্দেশে পাড়ি দেয়।

বোস ও বর্মন আজমীরগামী ট্রেনে মুকুল সমেত হাজরার সাক্ষাৎ পায়, ও
তাদের সঙ্গে আলাপ জমায়।

পরদিন জয়পুরে একটি কেল্লা দেখতে গিয়ে
তারা হাজরাকে সায়েস্তা করে। তারপর মুকুলের সঙ্গে ভাব জমিয়ে
তাকে সঙ্গে নিয়ে যোধপুরগামী ট্রেনে ওঠে।

যোধপুরে এসে ফেলু সার্কিট হাউসে ওঠে,
কারণ ডাঃ হাজরারও ওখানেই ওঠার কথা।
আসলে এখন বর্মন পালন করছেন হাজরার ভূমিকা,
আর মন্দার বোস সেজেছেন ভূপর্যটক। দুজনেই বোঝে ফেলুকে
খতম্ না করতে পারলে তাদের কার্যসিদ্ধি হবে না।

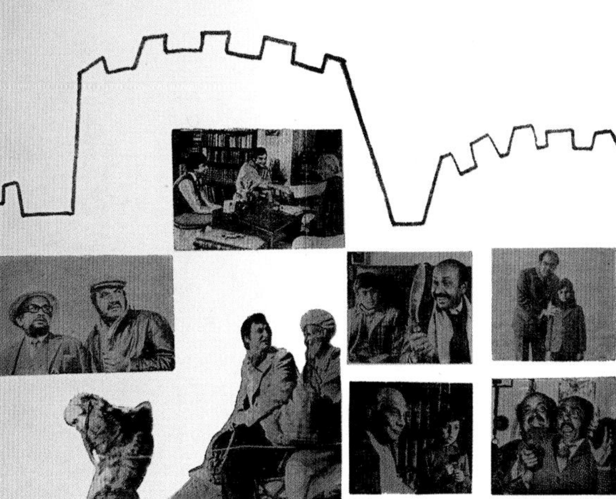

In Bookshelf
Encyclopaedias
Time-Table
Files
Magazines
Lamp (Goose-neck)
Typewriter
Inks
Scissors
Glue
Stapler
Desk Calendar
Reference books

LEFT PAGE: The draft (inset) and the detailed drawing of Feluda's bedroom for a scene in *Sonar Kella*
ABOVE AND LEFT: The detailed drawing and the draft of Feluda's drawing room where he meets his client in *Sonar Kella*

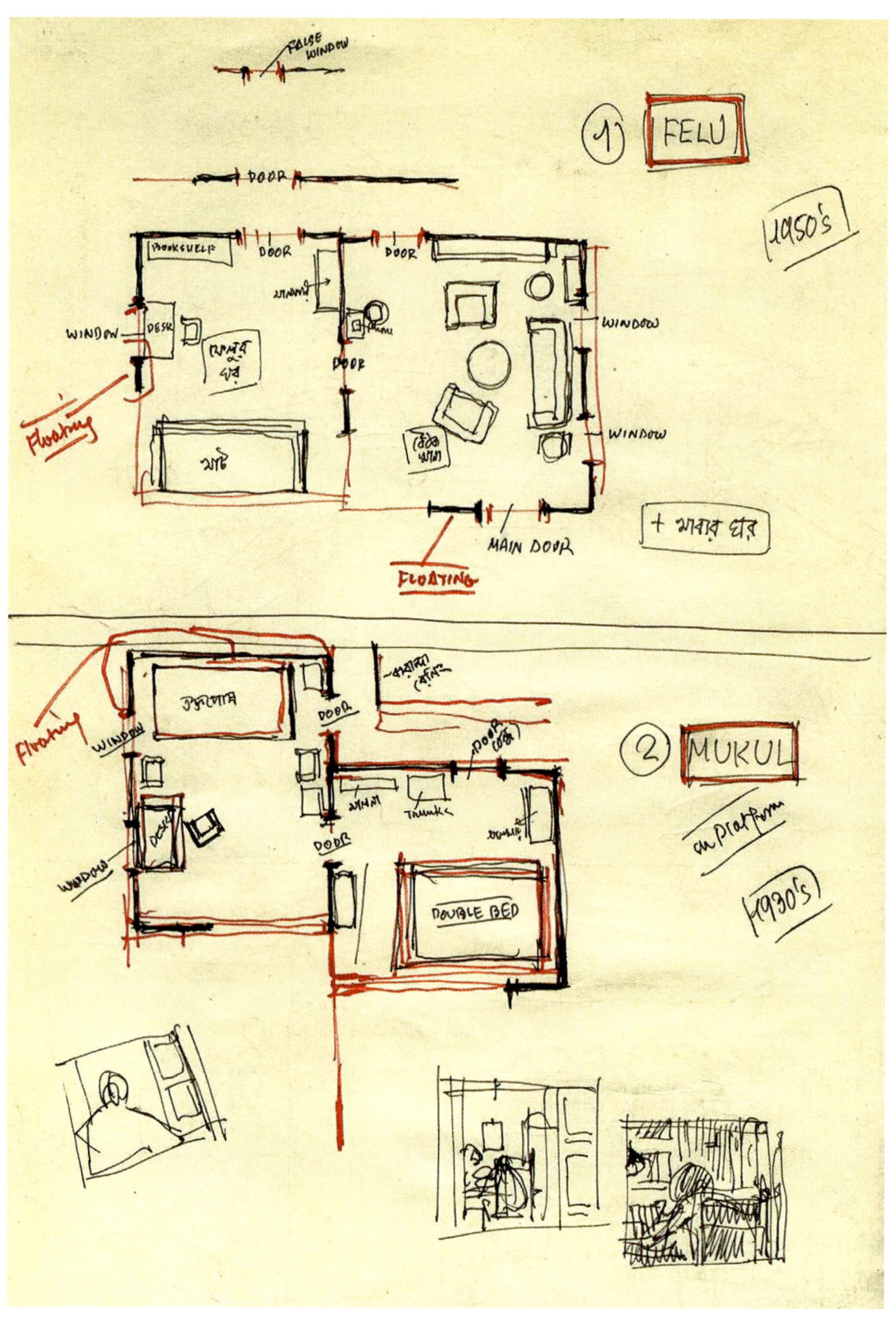

The plan of Feluda's home (with bedroom and drawing room) and Mukul's home drawn in meticulous detail by Ray

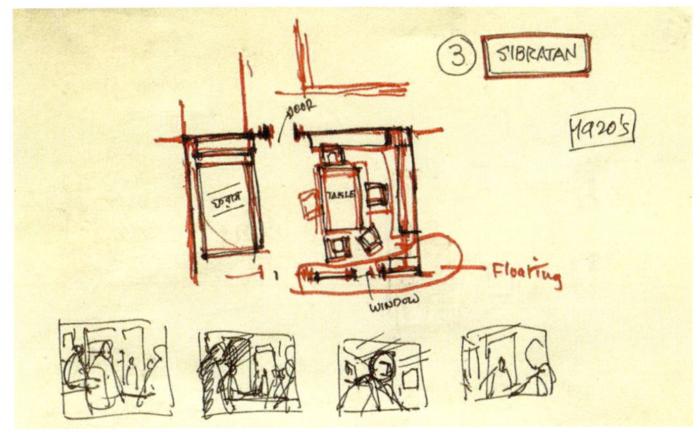

Left: The plan of Barrister Shibratan's house where Feluda meets the 'other' Mukul who was picked up 'by mistake'

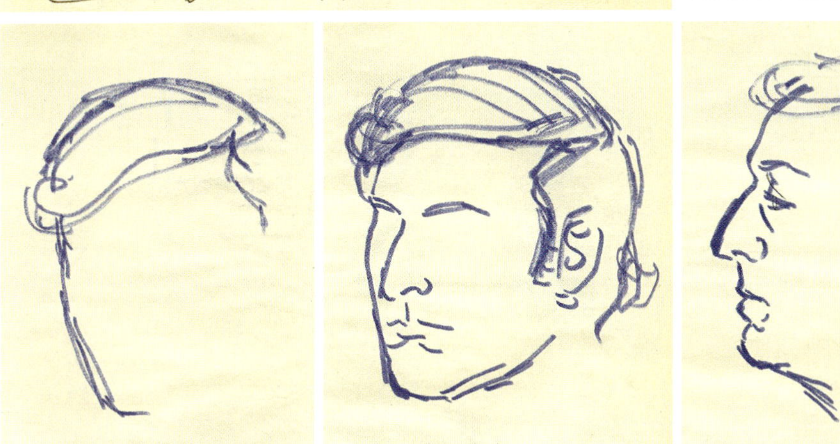

The evolution of Feluda's profile drawn by Ray is clearly based on the profile of Soumitra Chatterjee

Left: The character of the bumbling writer Lalmohan Ganguly (aka Jatayu) was introduced in *Sonar Kella*. The character, as drawn in the illustration of the book, changed completely with the casting of Santosh Dutta as Jatayu in the film. Ray's illustration of Santosh Dutta in *kheror khata* as Jatayu shows that change.

The detailing of Mandar Bose's profile by Ray

The inception of the fake Dr Hajra's character

The illustration of a traditional Rajasthani musician by Ray

Detailed ideas for clothing in *Sonar Kella*: Feluda

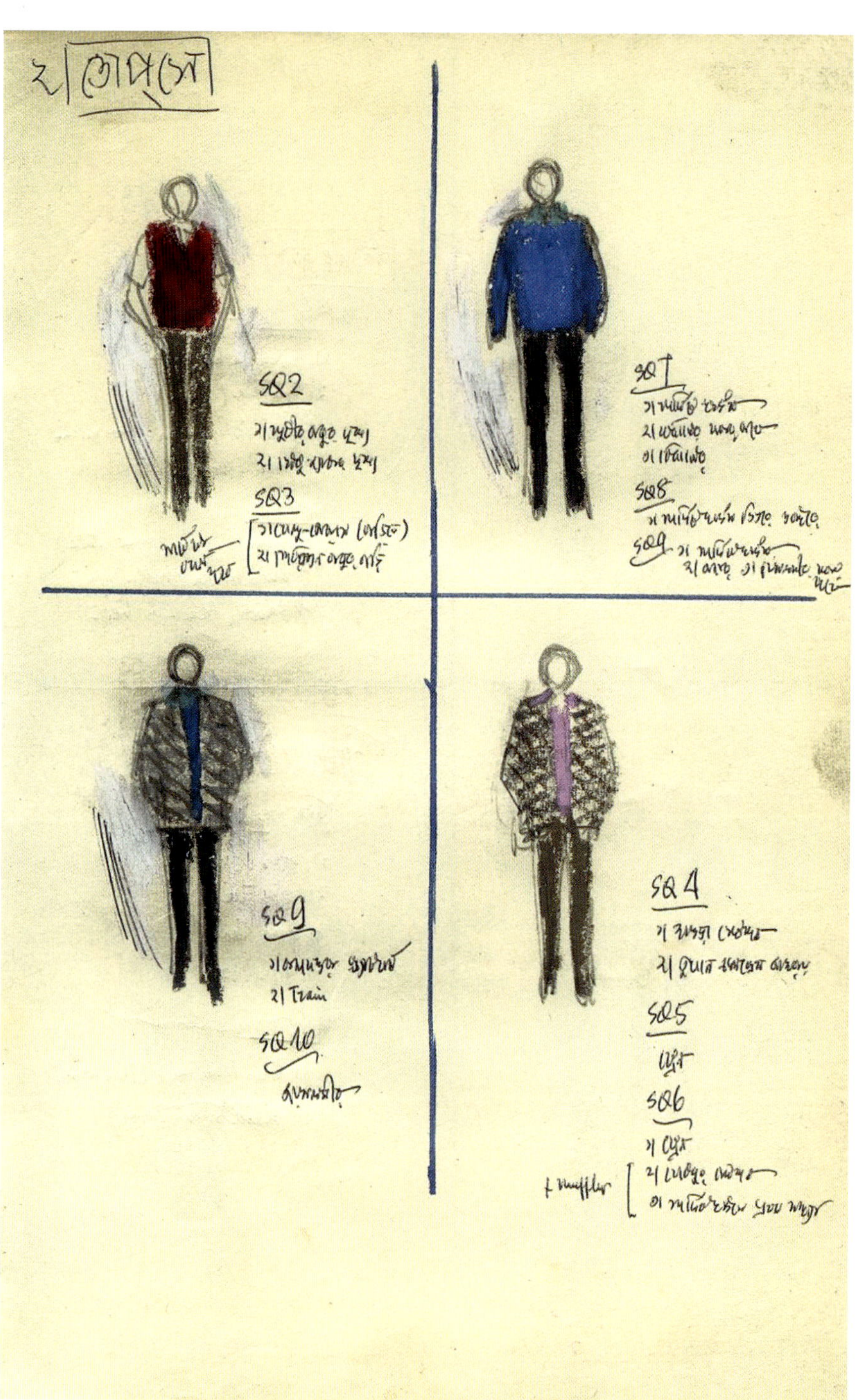

Detailed ideas for clothing in *Sonar Kella*: Topse

Detailed ideas for clothing in *Sonar Kella*: Mandar Bose (ABOVE) and Barman (BELOW)

Detailed ideas for clothing in *Sonar Kella*: Mukul

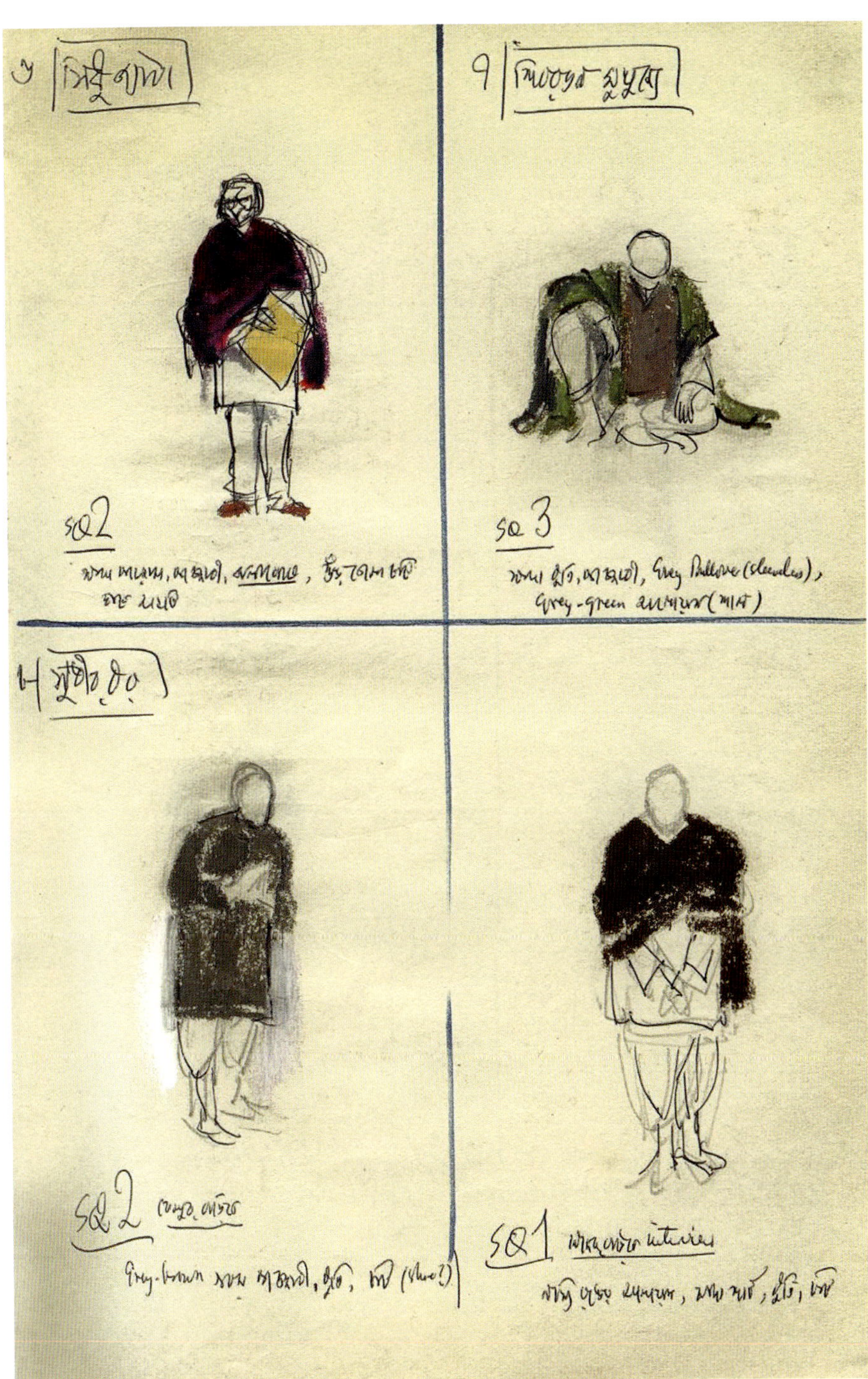

Detailed ideas for clothing in *Sonar Kella*: Sidhu *jetha*, Shibratan Mukherjee and Sudhir Dhar (CLOCKWISE FROM TOP LEFT)

Detailed ideas for clothing in *Sonar Kella*: Lalmohan Ganguly aka Jatayu

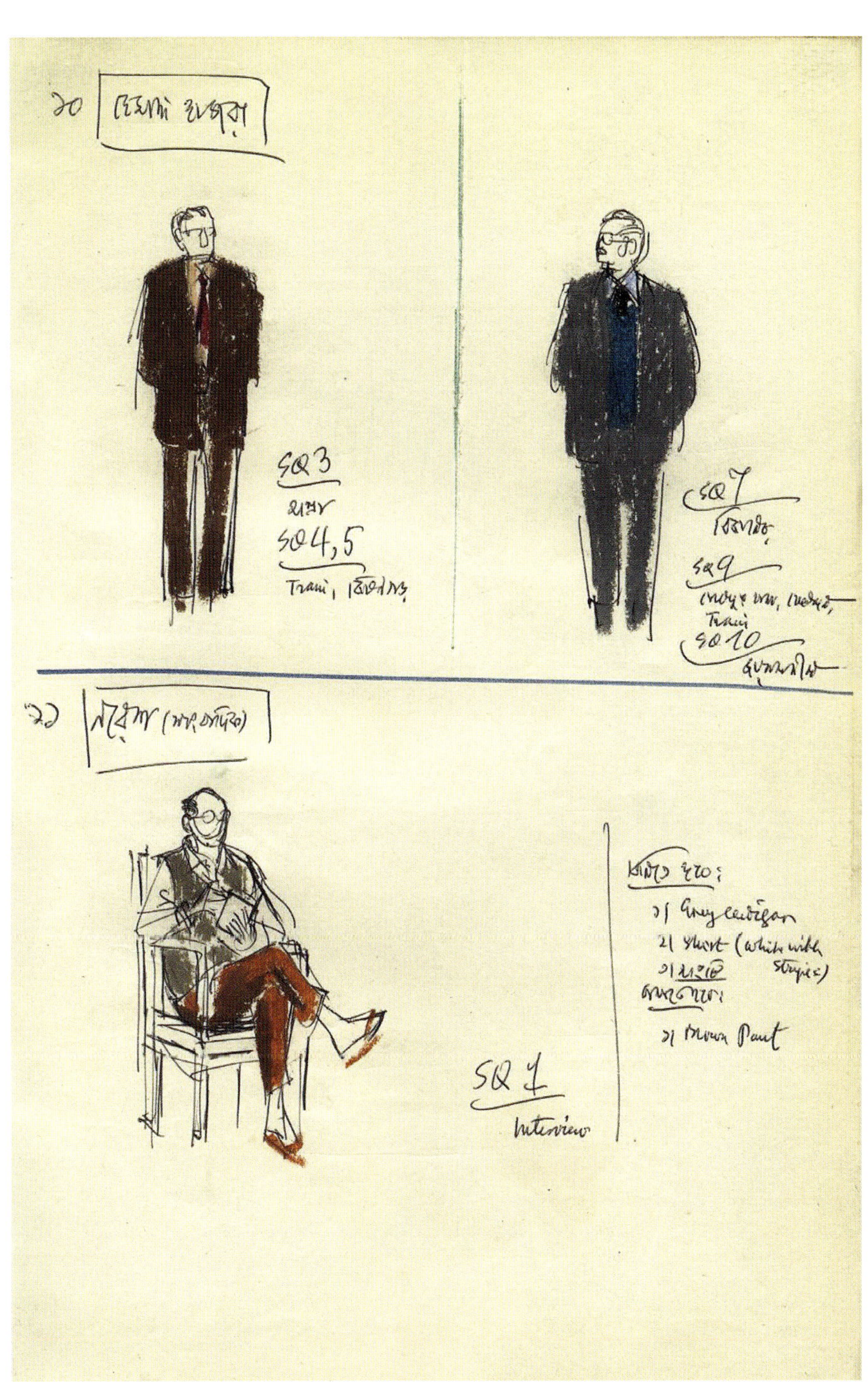

Detailed ideas for clothing in *Sonar Kella*: Dr Hemanga Hajra (ABOVE) and journalist Naresh (BELOW)

The dummy cover for Jatayu's potboiler created by Ray and Mayukh Chowdhury

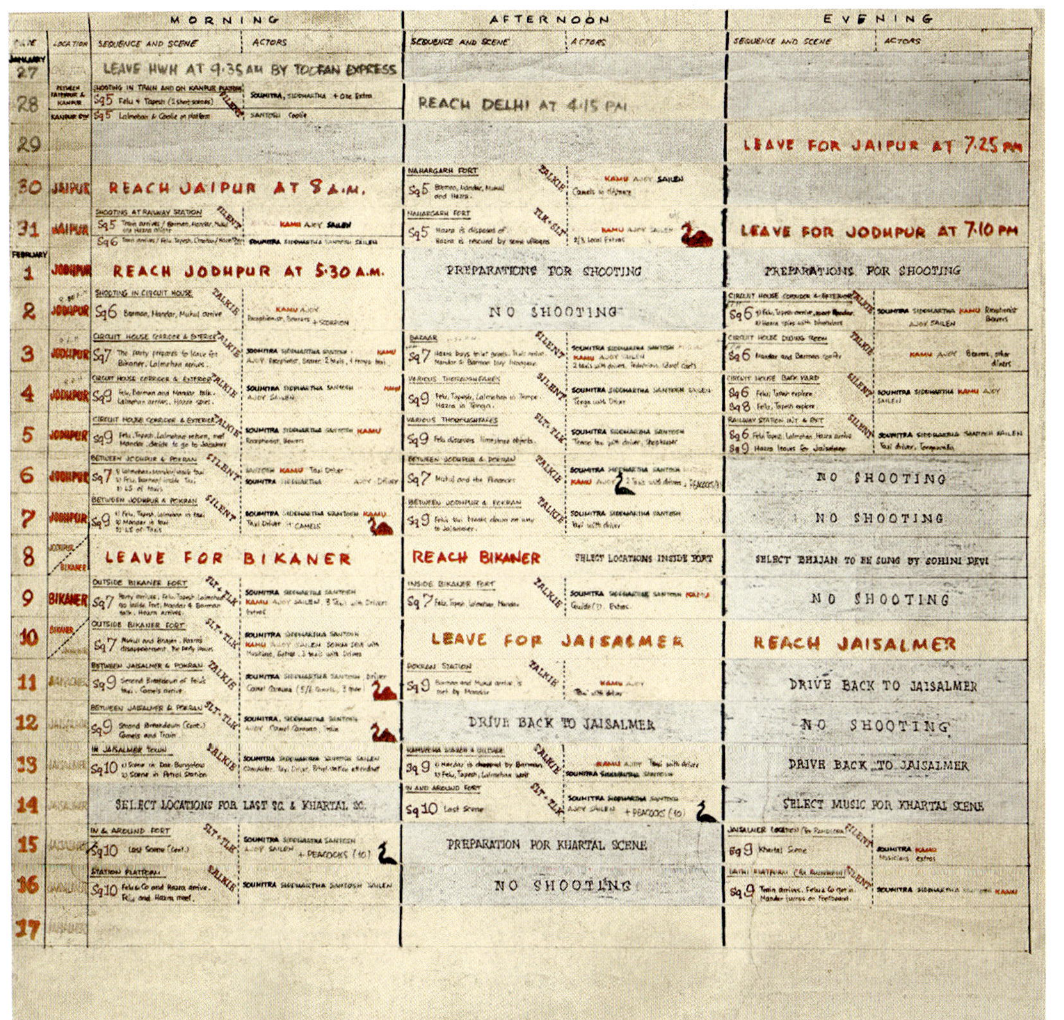

DATE	LOCATION	MORNING: SEQUENCE AND SCENE	MORNING: ACTORS	AFTERNOON: SEQUENCE AND SCENE	AFTERNOON: ACTORS	EVENING: SEQUENCE AND SCENE	EVENING: ACTORS
JANUARY 27		LEAVE HWH AT 9.35 AM BY TOOFAN EXPRESS					
28	BETWEEN [illegible] & KANPUR	SHOOTING IN TRAIN AND ON KANPUR PLATFORM Sq5 Felu + Topesh (2 short scenes) — SILENT	SOUMITRA, SIDDHARTHA + One Extra	REACH DELHI AT 4.15 PM			
	KANPUR STN	Sq5 Lalmohan & Coolie on platform	SANTOSH Coolie				
29						LEAVE FOR JAIPUR AT 7.25 PM	
30	JAIPUR	REACH JAIPUR AT 8 A.M.		NAHARGARH FORT Sq5 Barman, Mandar, Mukul and Hazra. — TALKIE	KAMU AJOY SAILEN Camels in distance		
31	JAIPUR	SHOOTING AT RAILWAY STATION Sq5 Train arrives / Barman, Mandar, Mukul [illegible] — SILENT	KAMU AJOY SAILEN	NAHARGARH FORT Sq5 Hazra is disposed of. Hazra is rescued by some villagers — TLK+SLT	KAMU AJOY SAILEN 2/3 Local Extras	LEAVE FOR JODHPUR AT 7.10 PM	
		Sq6 Train arrives / Felu, Topesh, [illegible]	SOUMITRA SIDDHARTHA SANTOSH SAILEN				
FEBRUARY 1	JODHPUR	REACH JODHPUR AT 5.30 A.M.		PREPARATIONS FOR SHOOTING		PREPARATIONS FOR SHOOTING	
2	JODHPUR	SHOOTING IN CIRCUIT HOUSE Sq6 Barman, Mandar, Mukul arrive — TALKIE	KAMU AJOY Receptionist, Bearers + SCORPION	NO SHOOTING		CIRCUIT HOUSE CORRIDOR & EXTERIOR Sq6 1) Felu, Topesh arrive, [illegible] 2) Hazra [illegible] — TALKIE	SOUMITRA SIDDHARTHA KAMU Receptionist Bearers AJOY SAILEN
3	JODHPUR	CIRCUIT HOUSE CORRIDOR & EXTERIOR Sq7 The party prepares to leave for Bikaner. Lalmohan arrives. — TALKIE	SOUMITRA SIDDHARTHA SANTOSH KAMU AJOY Receptionist, Bearer, 2 taxis, 1 tempo [illegible]	BAZAAR Sq7 Hazra buys [illegible] Mandar & Barman buy [illegible] — SILENT	SOUMITRA SIDDHARTHA SANTOSH KAMU AJOY SAILEN 2 taxis with drivers, [illegible]	CIRCUIT HOUSE DINING ROOM Sq6 Mandar and Barman [illegible] — TALKIE	KAMU AJOY Bearers, other diners
4	JODHPUR	CIRCUIT HOUSE CORRIDOR & EXTERIOR Sq9 Felu, Barman and Mandar talk. Lalmohan arrives. Hazra spies. — TALKIE	SOUMITRA SIDDHARTHA SANTOSH KAMU AJOY SAILEN	VARIOUS THOROUGHFARES Sq9 Felu, Topesh, Lalmohan in Tempo. Hazra in Tonga. — SILENT	SOUMITRA SIDDHARTHA SANTOSH SAILEN Tonga with Driver	CIRCUIT HOUSE BACK YARD Sq6 Felu, Topesh explore Sq8 Felu, Topesh explore — SILENT	SOUMITRA SIDDHARTHA KAMU AJOY SAILEN
5	JODHPUR	CIRCUIT HOUSE CORRIDOR & EXTERIOR Sq9 Felu, Topesh, Lalmohan return, meet Mandar, decide to go to Jaisalmer — TALKIE	SOUMITRA SIDDHARTHA SANTOSH KAMU Receptionist, Bearers	VARIOUS THOROUGHFARES Sq9 Felu discovers [illegible] objects. — SLT, TLK	SOUMITRA SIDDHARTHA SANTOSH Tempo [illegible] driver, Shopkeeper	RAILWAY STATION INT & EXT Sq6 Felu, Topesh, Lalmohan, Hazra arrive Sq9 Hazra leaves for Jaisalmer — SILENT	SOUMITRA SIDDHARTHA SANTOSH SAILEN Taxi driver, [illegible]
6	JODHPUR	BETWEEN JODHPUR & POKRAN Sq7 1) Lalmohan, Mandar inside taxi 2) Felu, Barman inside Taxi 3) LS of taxis — SILENT	SANTOSH KAMU Taxi Driver SOUMITRA SIDDHARTHA AJOY Driver	BETWEEN JODHPUR & POKRAN Sq7 Mukul and the Peacocks — TALKIE	SOUMITRA SIDDHARTHA SANTOSH KAMU AJOY 2 Taxis with drivers, PEACOCKS	NO SHOOTING	
7	JODHPUR	BETWEEN JODHPUR & POKRAN Sq9 1) Felu, Topesh, Lalmohan in taxi 2) Mandar in taxi 3) LS of Taxis — SILENT	SOUMITRA SIDDHARTHA SANTOSH KAMU Taxi Driver + CAMELS	BETWEEN JODHPUR & POKRAN Sq9 Felu's taxi breaks down on way to Jaisalmer. — TALKIE	SOUMITRA SIDDHARTHA SANTOSH Taxi with driver	NO SHOOTING	
8	JODHPUR / BIKANER	LEAVE FOR BIKANER		REACH BIKANER	SELECT LOCATIONS INSIDE FORT	SELECT BHAJAN TO BE SUNG BY SOHINI DEVI	
9	BIKANER	OUTSIDE BIKANER FORT Sq7 Party arrives, Felu, Topesh, Lalmohan go inside Fort, Mandar & Barman talk, Hazra arrives. — SLT + TLK	SOUMITRA SIDDHARTHA SANTOSH KAMU AJOY SAILEN, 3 Taxis with Drivers Extras	INSIDE BIKANER FORT Sq7 Felu, Topesh, Lalmohan, Mandar — TALKIE	SOUMITRA SIDDHARTHA SANTOSH KAMU Guide (?) Extras	NO SHOOTING	
10	BIKANER / [illegible]	OUTSIDE BIKANER FORT Sq7 Mukul and Bhajan, Hazra's disappointment, the party leaves — SLT + TLK	SOUMITRA SIDDHARTHA SANTOSH KAMU AJOY SAILEN SOHINI DEVI with Musicians, Extras, 3 taxis with Drivers	LEAVE FOR JAISALMER		REACH JAISALMER	
11	JAISALMER	BETWEEN JAISALMER & POKRAN Sq9 Second Breakdown of Felu's taxi, Camels arrive — TALKIE	SOUMITRA SIDDHARTHA SANTOSH Driver Camel Caravan (5/6 Camels, 3 [illegible])	POKRAN STATION Sq9 Barman and Mukul arrive, is met by Mandar — TALKIE	KAMU AJOY Taxi with driver	DRIVE BACK TO JAISALMER	
12	JAISALMER	BETWEEN JAISALMER & POKRAN Sq9 Second Breakdown (Cont.) Camels and Train — SLT + TLK	SOUMITRA, SIDDHARTHA SANTOSH AJOY Camel Caravan, Train	DRIVE BACK TO JAISALMER		NO SHOOTING	
13	JAISALMER	IN JAISALMER TOWN Sq10 1) Scene in Dak Bungalow 2) Scene in Petrol Station — TALKIE	SOUMITRA SIDDHARTHA SANTOSH SAILEN Chowkidar, Taxi Driver, Petrol station attendant	[illegible] Sq9 1) Mandar is [illegible] by Barman 2) Felu, Topesh, Lalmohan [illegible] — TALKIE	KAMU AJOY Taxi with driver SOUMITRA SIDDHARTHA SANTOSH	DRIVE BACK TO JAISALMER	
14	JAISALMER	SELECT LOCATIONS FOR LAST SC. & KHARTAL SC.		IN AND AROUND FORT Sq10 Last Scene — SLT + TLK	SOUMITRA SIDDHARTHA SANTOSH AJOY SAILEN + PEACOCKS (10)	SELECT MUSIC FOR KHARTAL SCENE	
15	JAISALMER	IN & AROUND FORT Sq10 Last Scene (Cont.) — SLT + TLK	SOUMITRA SIDDHARTHA SANTOSH AJOY SAILEN + PEACOCKS (10)	PREPARATION FOR KHARTAL SCENE		JAISALMER LOCATION (In Ramdevra) Sq9 Khartal Scene — SILENT	SOUMITRA KAMU Musicians extras
16	JAISALMER	STATION PLATFORM Sq10 Felu & Co and Hazra arrive. Felu and Hazra meet. — TALKIE	SOUMITRA SIDDHARTHA SANTOSH SAILEN	NO SHOOTING		[illegible] PLATFORM [illegible] Sq9 Train arrives. Felu & Co get in. Mandar jumps on footboard. — SILENT	SOUMITRA SIDDHARTHA [illegible] KAMU
17	JAISALMER						

The detailed shooting schedule drawn up by Ray in the pre-production stage

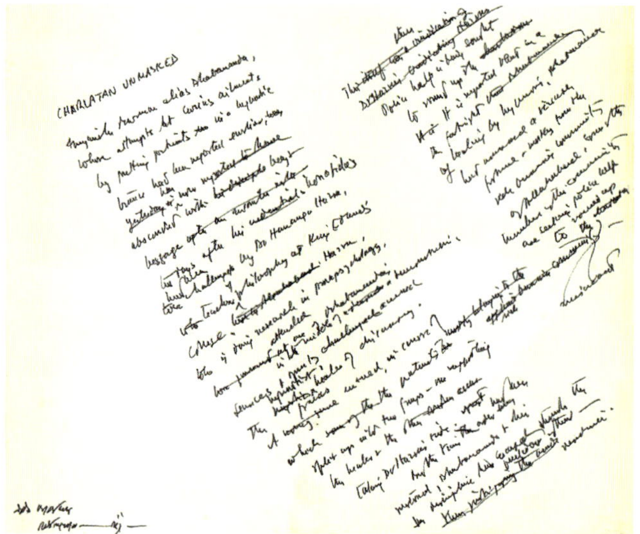

Charlatan Unmasked

ALLAHABAD, 1962.- Amiyanath Barman alias Bhabananda, whose attempts at caring ailments by putting patients in a hypnotic trance had been reported earlier, has now absconded with bags and baggage, two days after his 'bonafides' had been challenged by Dr. Hemanga Hazra, teacher of philosophy at King Edward's College. Hazra, who is doing research in parapsychology, attended one of Bhabananda's séances, and in the middle of a therapy session openly accused the hypnotic healer of chicanery. A fracas ensued in course of which the patients split up into two groups – one supporting the healer and the other taking Dr. Hazra's side. By the time order has been restored; Bhabananda and his disciple had escaped through the back door of their residence.

Police help is being sought to round up the absconders. It is reported that in a fortnight of healing by hypnosis, Bhabananda had assumed a sizeable fortune – mainly from the rich Marwari community of Allahabad. Some of the members of the community are seeking police help to round up the niscreants.

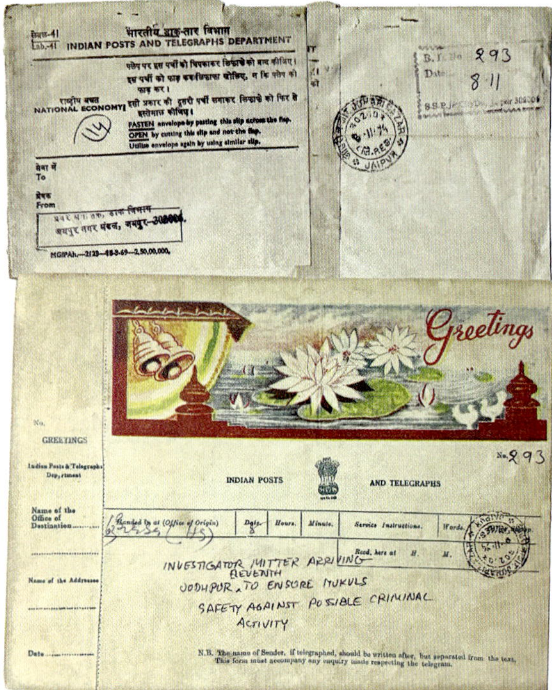

WEST BENGAL PARAPSYCHOLOGICAL SOCIETY

ANNIVERSARY CELEBRATION

PROGRAMME

1. Opening Song
2. Welcome address by Sri B. Chatterjee
3. "Mangalacharam" - Acharyya Karunamoy Saraswati
4. Inaguration by Sri Dakshina Ranjan Bose
5. Address by Chief Guest - Prof. H. N. Banerjee
6. Address by Dr. Bhupal Bose
7. Felicitation by—
   Sri Manindra N. Banerjee
   Sri Probodh Ch. Sinha
   Sri Satyajit Roy
   Dr. B. P. Kedia
   Sri Mohon K. Mookerjee
   Prof Manindra Chakrabarty
   Sm Rekha Chatterjee
8. Address
9. Speech by Mr. P. B. Mukherjee
10. Presidential Address
11. Devotional Song by Sri Acchutananda Brahmachari
12. Closing Song by Sm Dipti Banerjee

On Sunday 26th April, 1970
116, Dr. Lalmohon Bhattacharjee Road,
Entally, Calcutta - 14.

ENROL YOURSELF A MEMBER OF THE SOCIETY.

The draft text for the newspaper item was unused in *Sonar Kella* (ABOVE) and the telegram used in the film (BELOW LEFT); Ray's name featured prominently in the invitation card of the West Bengal Parapsychological Society (BELOW RIGHT).

কেল্লার সামনে যুদ্ধের এই ছবি শ্রীমান মুকুল ধর তার পুর্বজন্মের স্মৃতির উপর নির্ভর করে এঁকেছে বলে দাবী করে।

মুকুল ধর কি জাতিস্মর?

বিশেষ সংবাদদাতা

গড়পার রোডের একটি পুরনো বাড়ির বাইরের ঘরে সেদিন সকালে এক রহস্যের উদ্ঘাটন হল। সেই ঘরটির আসবাবপত্র সাধারণ-একটি সতরঞ্চি বিছানো তক্তপোষ, চেয়ার একটি টেবিল, একটি কাঠের আলমারি। সেই আলমারির সামনে একটি বেতের মোড়ায় চুপচাপ বসে রয়েছে ৮।৯ বছরের একটি ছেলে। তার নাম মুকুল ধর। মুকুলের চেহারায় বেশ সপ্রতিভ ভাব, তীক্ষ্ণ নাক, উজ্জ্বল অথচ স্বপ্নিল চোখ, গায়ের রং গৌর। কথা সে কম বলে। আমাদের পশ্নের উত্তরে মুকুল কাটছাঁট জবাব দিচ্ছিল। কিন্তু যখনই কথা বলে, তখন সে এই বিংশ শতাব্দীর কলকাতা শহরের একটি মধ্যবিত্ত পরিবারের ছেলে নয়-সেই মুহুর্তে মুকুল বিগত কালের রাজস্থানের বালক; তার সময় সুদুর কোন ঐতিহাসিক কালে বিস্তৃত। সেই জন্মের প্রতিটি স্মৃতি তাকে এজন্মে আচ্ছন্ন করে রেখেছে।

মুকুলের বাবার নাম সুধীর ধর। তাঁর আরও একটি ছেলে ও একটি মেয়ে রয়েছে; মুকুল সর্বাপেক্ষা কনিষ্ঠ। কলেজ স্ট্রীটে ধর মহাশয়ের বইয়ের ব্যবসা রয়েছে। সুধীরবাবুর কথায় জানা গেল, মাস দু-তিন ধরে তাঁরা এই গতজন্মের স্মৃতিচারণের ব্যাপারটা লক্ষ্য করছেন। মুকুলের নেশা ছবি আঁকা; সুধীরবাবু বললেন, 'সে সব ছবির সাবজেকটও রাজস্থানের সিনসিনারি।' প্রশ্ন করলাম, ছবির বিষয় কি পার্টিকুলার কোনো ঘটনা বা মানুষকে কেন্দ্র করে? সুধীরবাবু এক বান্ডিল ছবি এগিয়ে দিলেন, 'দেখুন না-ও সারাক্ষণই আঁকে।' সেই রঙিন ছবিগুলিতে মরুভূমি, বালি, ছোটখাটো পাহাড়, ময়ুর, কেল্লা আছে- কিছু যুদ্ধের দৃশ্যও রয়েছে। ছবিগুলি দেখলে হঠাৎ অবাক হতে হয়- কোনো জায়গা বা ঘটনার এমন স্পষ্ট অনুভুতি চাক্ষুষ অভিজ্ঞতা ছাড়া সম্ভব নয়। অথচ সুধীরবাবু জানালেন, 'মুকুল জন্মাবধি, রাজস্থান দুরের কথা, কাছাকাছি কোথাও যায়নি।' তবে কি সমস্ত ঘটনা তার গত জীবনের সুস্পষ্ট প্রভাব?

তারপরে আমরা প্রশ্ন করি, মুকুলকে। 'কবে ছিলে ওখানে?' আমাদের এই প্রশ্নের উত্তরে মুকুল ঠিক সময়টা বলতে পারে না, অন্য কথায় চলে যায়। সে জানায়, সে যুদ্ধ দেখেছে। তারপরের প্রশ্নের উত্তর মুকুল বিস্ময়করভাবে দিল যে, সে যুদ্ধে যোগ দেয়নি, কারণ 'আমি ত ছোট ছিলাম।'

তার চেয়েও চমকপ্রদ ব্যাপার তার কথাবার্তায় জানা যায়। একটি আংটি দেখে তার নিজের আংটির কথা মনে পড়ে-আমরা প্রশ্নের সুত্র ধরে জানতে পারি যে, সে অজস্র ছোট ছোট লাল নীল সবুজ রঙের উজ্জ্বল পাথর দেখেছে। আমাদের সন্দেহ নেই যে, মুকুল দামী রত্নের কথাই বলছে। এইসব মুল্যবান রত্ন যে মুকুলের বাড়িতেই কোনো গোপন স্থানে রক্ষিত ছিল, সে বিষয়ও কোনো সন্দেহের অবকাশ নেই। এই গুপ্তধনের ইঙ্গিতই শ্রীমান মুকুলের স্মৃতিচারণের সবচেয়ে রোমাঞ্চকর ও চিত্তাকর্ষক অংশ।

সুধীর ধর মহাশয় জানালেন, বিখ্যাত প্যারাসাইকোলজিস্ট ডঃ হেমাঙ্গ হাজরা শিগগিরই শ্রীমান মুকুলসহ রাজস্থান রওনা হবেন। এই পরিকল্পনায় মুকুল নিজে অত্যান্ত উৎসাহী দেখা গেল। শ্রীমান মুকুলের রাজস্থান ভ্রমণ পরামনোবিজ্ঞান বিভাগে নতুন দিগন্তের সুচনা করে কিনা দেখবার জন্য আমরাও উৎসাহী।

The newspaper facsimile featuring the news of Mukul’s reincarnation created specifically for the film

The lobby cards of *Sonar Kella* featuring production stills taken by Nemai Ghosh

Vignettes from the outdoor shoot of the kidnapping scene in the by-lanes of Kolkata. Both photographs are taken by Sandip Ray.

Candid shots behind the scenes. Both photographs are taken by Sandip Ray.

The scene deleted from the final cut of *Sonar Kella* (Above); the hands of Mandar Bose in the iconic train scene were really Ray's hands as seen in the photograph (Below). Both photographs are taken by Sandip Ray.

Behind the scenes candids during the shooting of the film: Soumitra Chatterjee and Siddhartha Chatterjee, as Feluda and Topse, respectively, had a wonderful camaraderie that helped to recreate the iconic characters from the novel (Top Left and Left); Ajoy Banerjee as the fake Dr Hajra and Kushal Chakraborty as Mukul display contrasting moods during the shooting of the train scene (Top Right). The photographs used here are reproduced courtesy of Sandip Ray.

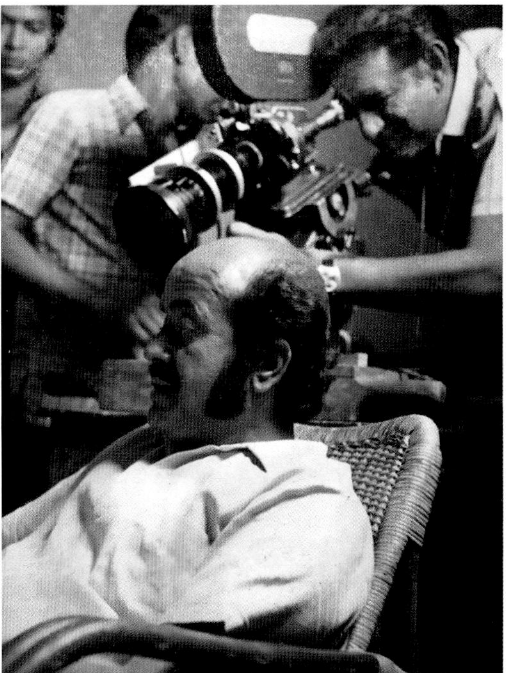

The many avatars of Kamu Mukherjee during the shooting of the film. All photographs are taken by Sandip Ray.

Cinematography played a crucial role in the film. The vibrant colours of Rajasthan gave ample opportunity to explore its palette.
The cinematographer Soumendu Roy played a crucial role in shaping the look of the film.
He is seen paying close attention to what Ray is saying as he makes notes in his draft book (LEFT);
Soumendu Roy shooting a scene from the film (BELOW).
The photographs used here are reproduced courtesy of Sandip Ray.

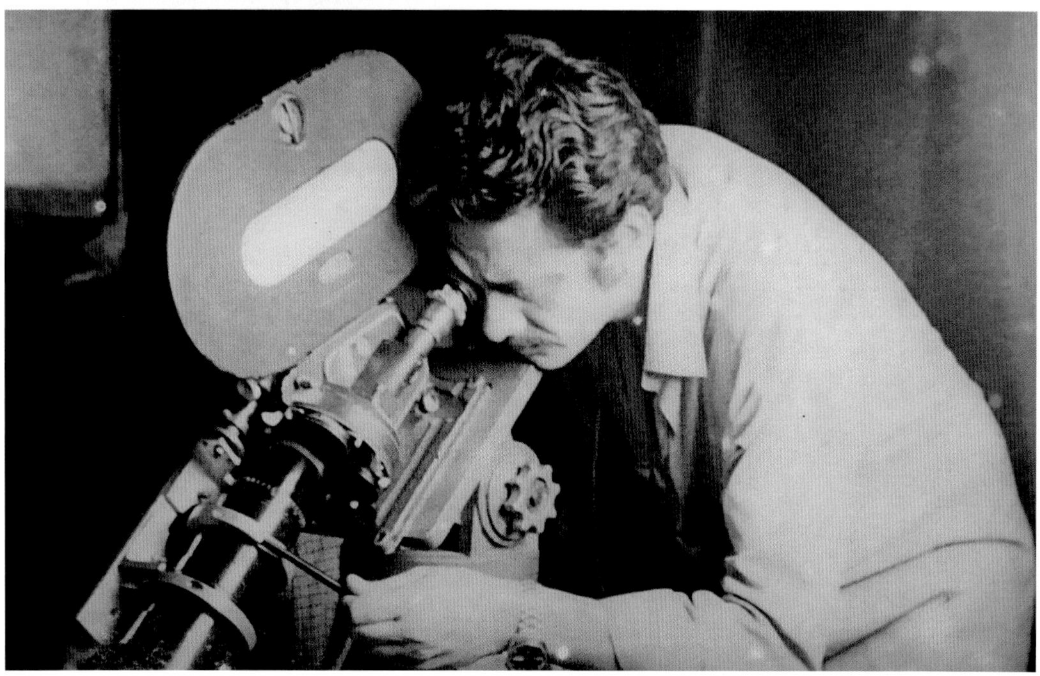

The colourful title cards of *Sonar Kella* illustrated by Ray

The colourful title cards of *Sonar Kella* illustrated by Ray

The colourful title cards of *Sonar Kella* illustrated by Ray

The colourful title cards of *Sonar Kella* illustrated by Ray

TEN

It was a passenger train running on meter gauge. Its compartments were therefore quite small. There were not many passengers, either; hence when we found an empty first-class compartment, it did not surprise me.

Inside the coach, it was dark. We groped for a switch, found it and pressed it—to no avail. Lalmohan Babu said, 'Bulbs in railway compartments tend to vanish even in civilized areas. In this land of bandits, one shouldn't even expect to find any!'

'The two of you can take the benches. I will spread a durrie on the floor and manage. We have six whole hours in hand—time enough for a nice, long nap!' said Feluda.

Lalmohan Babu raised a mild objection to this plan, 'Why should you be on the floor? Let me...!' But Feluda said, 'Certainly not!' so sternly that he said nothing more. I saw him spread his holdall on one of the benches, not merely because of Feluda's words, but perhaps also out of concern for his aching joints.

The train began pulling out of the platform. Within a minute of leaving the station, suddenly a figure jumped on to the footboard of our carriage. Lalmohan Babu said with a laugh, 'Hey, this is a reserved compartment. Ladies only!'

Then the door swung open quickly, and a bright light from a torch dazzled our eyes for a few seconds. We saw a hand coming towards us. The point of a gun shone in that light. All of us raised our arms high above our heads.

'Get up, dear hearts! The door's open, get out of the train. All of you!' It was the voice of Mandar Bose.

'But...but the train's still running!' said Lalmohan Babu in a trembling voice.

'Shut up!' roared Mandar Bose and inched a little closer. The torchlight was playing on our faces constantly, never standing still for more than a few moments.

'You trying to be funny?' Mr Bose went on. 'What do you do in Calcutta? Don't you climb in and out running buses? Get up, I tell you!'

Just as he finished speaking, something happened so totally unexpectedly that it took my breath away. I shall never forget it as long as I live. Feluda's right arm came down in a flash. He grasped a corner of the durrie and yanked it off the floor. As a result, Mandar Bose lost his balance. His feet slipped, then rose in the air for a second, before he fell, the top half of his body hitting the wall of the carriage with a bang. At the same time, the revolver was knocked out of his hand. It fell on Lalmohan Babu's bench, and the torch dropped from his left hand on to the floor.

All that happened in a split second. Even before Mandar Bose crashed down on the floor, Feluda had sprung up, clutching his own revolver, which had come out of his jacket pocket.

'Get up!' This time it was Feluda who ordered Mandar Bose.

The meter gauge train was swinging and swaying across the desert, making a lot of noise. Lalmohan Babu had, in the meantime, grabbed Mr Bose's revolver and stuffed it into his own Japan Airlines bag.

'Get up!' Feluda shouted again.

The torch was rolling on the floor. I could see that it should really be focussed on Mr Bose, or the fellow might take advantage of the darkness and try to trick us. Some such thought made me bend down to pick it up—which led to disaster. Even now, my blood runs cold when I think about it.

Mandar Bose was facing my bench. Just as I bent down, he suddenly lunged forward, grabbed me and got to his feet, holding me firmly in front of himself. As a result, I became a protective shield for him. Even at such a critical moment, I couldn't help admiring his cunning. It was clear that although round one had gone to Feluda most unexpectedly, he was certainly in a difficult position in the second round. And I was wholly to blame.

Mandar Bose kept a tight hold on me as he began moving towards the open door. I could feel something sharp hurting my shoulder. Then I realized it was one of his nails. Suddenly, I remembered little Neelu complaining that his hand hurt.

We were now standing very close to the door. I could feel the biting cold night air. It was brushing against my left shoulder.

Mandar Bose took another step. Feluda's gun was pointed at him, but now Feluda couldn't really do anything. The torch was still rolling on the floor as the train swayed from side to side. Suddenly, I was flung forward, with considerable force. It made me collide

Mandar Bose kept a tight hold on me as he began moving towards the open door.

with Feluda. The sound that came a second later told me that Mandar Bose had jumped out of the moving train. What I could not tell was whether he had survived or not.

Feluda went to the door and peered out. He came back a couple of minutes later, replaced his revolver and said, 'I hope he breaks a few bones, or it will be a matter of great regret.'

Lalmohan Babu laughed—a trifle loudly—and said, 'Didn't I tell you the man was suspicious?'

I gulped some water from the flask. My heartbeat was gradually returning to normal, as was my breathing. I was still finding it difficult to grasp the enormity of what had just happened, in a matter of minutes.

'He got away this time only because of dear Topesh,' said Feluda, 'or I'd have used my gun to drag a full confession out of him. However...' he stopped. After a brief pause, he said, 'When I come face to face with danger, my brain starts working much more efficiently. I've noticed it before. Now I can see what that code meant.'

'Really?' Lalmohan Babu sounded amazed.

'It's actually quite simple. "I" is the man writing the note, "P" is Pokhran, "U" is "you", and "M" is "Mitter". Pradosh Mitter.'

'And the plus and minus signs?'

'IP 1625 + U. That means "I am arriving at Pokhran at 4.25. You must join me."'

'And U – M? What does that mean?'

'That's even simpler. It means "you get rid of Mitter".'

'Get rid . . .?' Lalmohan Babu could barely speak. 'You mean the minus sign stands for murder?'

'No, not necessarily. If you were forced to jump out of a moving train, chances are you'd be injured. And, in any case, you'd have to wait another twenty-four hours for the next train. The crooks would have finished their business in that time. What they really needed to do was stop us from going to Jaisalmer. That's why they littered the road with nails and pins. But when they realized that hadn't worked, Bose tried to get us off the train.'

Suddenly, I became aware of a smell. 'I can smell a cigar, Feluda!' I exclaimed.

'Yes, I got that smell as soon as the fellow jumped into the compartment. It was obvious even in the Circuit House that someone was smoking cigars. Remember that golden foil Mukul found? Cigars are wrapped in that kind of foil.'

'And there's something else. One of his nails is much longer than others. My shoulder must be as badly scratched as Neelu's hand.'

'All right, but who is the "I" who is giving all the instructions?'

Lalmohan Babu wanted to know.

Feluda's voice sounded solemn when he spoke. 'That warning someone had left for me in the Circuit House, and this handwritten code both point to one person.'

'Who?' Lalmohan Babu and I cried together.

'Dr Hemanga Mohan Hajra.'

The rest of the night passed without further excitement. I slept for about three hours. When I woke, it was bright and sunny outside. Feluda was no longer lying on the floor. He was seated in one corner of my bench and staring out of the window. On his lap was his blue notebook, and in his hands were two notes. One was the warning, and the other was the letter Dr Hajra had left for us before leaving Jodhpur. I glanced at my watch. It was a quarter to seven. Lalmohan Babu was still fast asleep. I felt very hungry, but had no wish to eat another goja. We would reach Jaisalmer at nine. Somehow, I must put up with the pangs of hunger until then.

The scenery outside was really strange. For mile after mile stretched an undulating landscape—there was not a single house in sight, not a single human being, not even a tree. Yet I could not call it a desert because, although there was a little sand, most of it consisted of dry, pale grass, reddish earth and blackish-red chips of stone. It seemed incredible that, after such a landscape, we would find a whole town again.

The train stopped at a station called Jetha-chandan. I opened the railway timetable and discovered that the next station was called Thaiyat Hamira, and the one after that was Jaisalmer. At Jethachandan, there were no shops or stalls on the platform, no hawkers, no porters, no passengers. It was as if our train had somehow arrived at a place that had not yet been discovered by man. It was no different from a rocket landing on moon.

Lalmohan Babu woke soon after the train started moving again. He yawned and said, 'I had the most fantastic dream, you know. There was this gang of bandits, each with a moustache that looked like the horns of a ram. I had hypnotized them, and was leading them through a castle. There was a tunnel. We went through the tunnel and reached an underground chamber. I knew there was some treasure buried in that chamber, but all I could see was a camel sitting on the floor, chewing *gojas*!'

'How do you know that?' Feluda asked. 'Did the camel open its mouth and show you what it was chewing?'

'No, no. But I saw my tin—there it was, lying in front of the camel!'

Soon after we left Thaiyat Hamira, in the distance, the hazy outline of a hill came into view. It was a Rajasthani table mountain with a flat top. Our train appeared to be going in that direction.

Around eight o'clock, we could dimly see some sort of structure on top of that hill. Slowly, it became clear that it was a fortress. It stood like a crown atop the hill, spread all around its flattened top. It was bathed in the bright light of the early morning sun, which was falling directly upon it from a dazzling sky. Quite involuntarily, three words slipped out of my mouth: 'The golden fortress!'

'That's right,' Feluda told me. 'This is the only golden fortress in Rajasthan. That bowl in that shop in Jodhpur raised my suspicions.

Then I looked it up in the guide book, and my suspicions were confirmed. The fort and the bowl were both made with the same stone—yellow sandstone. If Mukul is truly a *jatismar*, and if there is truly something like a previous life, then I think he was born somewhere in this region.'

'But does Dr Hajra know that?' I asked.

Feluda did not reply. He was still staring at the fort. 'You know something, Topshe?' he said finally. 'There is something special about that golden light. It has helped me see the whole pattern of the spider's web, very clearly!'

ELEVEN

The first thing we did on getting off the train in Jaisalmer was to stop at a tea stall and have a cup of tea and some sweets. It was a new kind of sweet, one that we hadn't had before. Feluda said it would do us good as it had glucose in it. A lot of activity lay ahead, the glucose would provide extra energy.

We emerged from the station to find that there was not a single vehicle we could hire—no tongas, ekkas, cycle-rickshaws, or taxis. There was a jeep waiting, but it was obviously not meant for hire. When we got off the train, I had noticed a black Ambassador standing outside. But now even that had gone.

'It's a small town,' Feluda said. 'I don't think a place is all that far from another. My guide book says there's a dak bungalow. Let's go and find it.'

We set off, carrying our luggage. Soon enough, we found a petrol station, where a man gave us directions. In order to get to the dak bungalow, we would not have to climb the hill, he said. The bungalow was located on the plains, to the south of the hill. As we began walking again, Feluda looked at the tyre marks on the sand and said, 'That Ambassador must have come this way!'

About fifteen minutes later, we came upon a bungalow. A wooden board fixed to its gate told us that we had come to the right place. The black Ambassador was parked in front of it. An old man wearing a khaki shirt and a short dhoti came out of an outhouse. On his head was a turban. Perhaps he had seen us arrive. Feluda asked him in Hindi if he was the chowkidar. The man nodded. It appeared from the way he was looking at us that our arrival was unexpected, and he didn't altogether approve of our sudden appearance, as no one was allowed to stay in the bungalow without prior permission.

Feluda said nothing about staying there. All we wanted to do, he told the man, was leave our luggage in the bungalow. Then we'd try to get the necessary permission. 'You'll have to see the Raja's secretary for that,' said the chowkidar and pointed us in the right direction.

The palace, also made of yellow sandstone, was at some distance; but certain portions of it were visible, rising above the trees. The chowkidar raised no objection to our luggage being left there. He showed us into a small room, where we dumped our suitcases and holdalls. Then we filled our flasks with fresh water, slung them on our shoulders and asked him the way to the fort.

'You want to go to the fort?'

The question came from the far end of a passage. A gentleman had just come out of a room. He appeared no more than forty, had a clear complexion, and a sharp nose, under which was a thin moustache, very carefully trimmed. A second later, he was joined by an older man, who was clutching a stick—the kind that we had seen in the market in Jodhpur—and was wearing an odd, somewhat ill fitting black suit. I could not tell which part of the country they might be from. The second man was limping slightly, which explained the need for the stick.

'Yes, a look at the fort might be interesting,' said Feluda.

'Come along with us, we are going that way.'

Feluda thought for a few moments, then agreed. 'Thank you very much, it is very kind of you,' he said.

As we made our way to the car, Lalmohan Babu whispered into my ear: 'I hope these men won't try to throw us out of a moving car!'

The car began its journey to the fort. The man with the stick asked us, 'Are you from Calcutta?'

'Yes,' Feluda replied.

To our left, in the distance, rising from the sand, were stone pillars. We had seen something similar in Devikund. Feluda said such structures were quite common in Rajasthan.

Our car started going uphill. About a minute later, we heard another car. It was tooting urgently. That was a bit surprising, since we were not driving all that slowly and getting in its way. Feluda was sitting at the back with the two gentlemen. He turned round, peered through the glass and suddenly said to our driver, 'Stop! Please stop!'

Our car pulled up by the side of the road. At once, a taxi came along and stopped on our right. Holding its steering wheel was Gurbachan Singh, greeting us with a smile. The three of us climbed out. Feluda said to the two men, 'Thank you so much for your help. But this is our own taxi. It had broken down on the way to Jaisalmer, but now it's caught up with us.' When we were back in his car, Gurbachan told us how, at half past six that morning, he had spotted another taxi going back from Jaisalmer. He knew its driver, and managed to get a spare tyre from him. Then he covered ninety miles in two hours. When he reached Jaisalmer, he simply waited at the petrol station, until he spotted us inside the black Ambassador.

A little later, we found ourselves going through a market. There were shops everywhere, a loudspeaker was playing a Hindi song and, outside a small cinema, was a poster advertising a Hindi film.

'You want to see the fort?' Gurbachan asked.

'Yes,' Feluda told him. Gurbachan stopped the taxi and said, 'This is its gate.'

To our right was a massive gate, beyond which rose a road, paved with stone, which led to a second gate. That, I realized, was the real entrance to the fort, the first one acted as the front gate. Behind the entrance, rising steeply, was the golden fortress of Jaisalmer.

A guard was standing outside the front gate. Feluda went and asked him if he had seen a man with a small boy that morning. He indicated Mukul's height.

'Yes, sir, they were here. But they've now left,' replied the guard.

'When did they leave?'

'About half an hour ago.'

'Did they come by car?'

'Yes, sir. In a taxi.'

'Which way did they go? Can you remember?'

The guard nodded and pointed at the road that went further west. We got back to the car and followed it, passing through little alleys and more shops. Lalmohan Babu was sitting next to Gurbachan. Feluda and I were in the back seat. After a few minutes, Feluda suddenly asked, 'You didn't bring your weapon with you, did you?'

Startled by such a question, Lalmohan Babu said, 'The dodger?

No, sorry, I mean that Nepali dagger?'

'Yes, sir. Your dagger.'

'That's in my suitcase.'

'In that case, take out Mandar Bose's revolver from your Japan Airlines bag and tuck it into your belt. Make sure it isn't visible.'

From Lalmohan Babu's movements, it became clear that he was following Feluda's instruction. I was dying to see his face, but couldn't.

'Don't worry,' Feluda said reassuringly, 'If things get sticky, all you have to do is take that gun out and point it in front of you.'

'What if b-b-behind me, there's . . .?'

'If you hear a noise behind you, then just turn around. Then your "behind" will become your "front", see?'

'And you? Are you ... I mean, today, are you going to be non-violent?'

'That depends.'

Our taxi left the market behind and came to an open space. We had already asked a couple of men on the way, and learnt that the other taxi had been seen coming this way. Besides, we had also seen tyre-marks in the sand from time to time, which told us that we were following the same route that Dr Hemanga Hajra had taken. Gurbachan Singh came up with more information. 'This is the way to Mohangarh,' he said. 'I could drive for another mile, but after that the road gets really rough. Only jeeps can travel on that road, nothing else.'

But we didn't have to go another mile. Only a little later, we saw a taxi standing on one side of the road. To our right, at some distance, were a number of old, abandoned stone houses. All the roofs had caved in. Clearly, it had once been a village. We had seen similar villages elsewhere. People had moved out of them a long time ago. The walls of these houses were still standing only because they were made of stone.

We told Gurbachan to wait, and made our way to the houses. I saw Gurbachan get out of his car and go towards the other one, perhaps to chat with its driver.

Everything was eerily silent. If I turned my head, I could see the fort behind me, on top of the hill. Opposite the road, another hill rose steeply. At its foot, spread over a wide, open area were rows of yellow stones, embedded in the ground. They looked like giant spice grinders.

'Graves of warriors,' whispered Feluda.

Lalmohan Babu spoke, in a hoarse yet squeaky voice, 'I...I...have low blood pressure!'

'Don't you worry,' Feluda replied. 'It will soon rise higher, I promise you, and stop exactly where it should.'

We were now quite close to the houses. A path ran straight through them. I realized this village was different from the ones I had seen in Bengal. It had a simple, geometric plan.

But where were the people who had travelled in the other taxi? Where was Mukul? And Dr Hajra?

Had something happened to Mukul?

Suddenly, I became aware of a noise. It was faint, but audible if I strained my ears: thud, thud, thud, thud!

We walked on, very carefully and very silently. Then we reached a crossroad where two lanes intersected. The noise was coming from the right. Ten or twelve houses stood by the road. There were yawning gaps between their walls and where once there must have been doors.

We turned right and resumed walking stealthily.

Feluda uttered one word through his teeth, almost inaudibly, 'Revolver!' I saw that his hand had disappeared under his jacket. Out of the corner of my eye, I saw a revolver in Lalmohan Babu's hand, which was trembling violently.

A sudden crunching noise made us come to a halt. In the next instant, through the door of a house at the far end on our left, appeared Mukul, running fast. Then he saw us, ran even faster, and flung himself on Feluda's chest. He was gasping, his face was deathly pale.

I opened my mouth to ask him what had happened, but Feluda placed a finger on his lips and stopped me from speaking aloud.

'Please look after him until I return!' he whispered to Lalmohan Babu, and left Mukul in his charge. Then he proceeded towards the house from which we had just seen Mukul emerge. I followed Feluda.

The strange noise was getting louder. It sounded as if someone was lifting stones. Thud! Bang! Clang! It went on.

Feluda flattened himself against the wall as we got close to the house. A couple of

In the next instant, through the door of a house at the far end on our left, appeared Mukul, running fast.

steps later, we were able to peer through the gap left by the missing door. With his back to us, crouching over a huge pile of rubble, was Dr Hajra. Like a madman, he was removing stone after stone from that heap, and casting each one aside. He had no idea that we were standing so close.

Feluda took another step, pointing his revolver at Dr Hajra.

Suddenly, we heard a flutter above our heads.

A peacock swooped down from the compound wall. It sped towards Dr Hajra the instant it landed, and attacked him, pecking hard just under his left ear. Dr Hajra, who was still crouching over the stones, could only scream in agony and press his hand over that spot. At once, the white cuff of his shirt turned red.

But the peacock hadn't finished. It continued to attack him, pecking wherever it could. Dr Hajra turned, took a step towards the door in an attempt to escape, and saw us. He started as if he'd seen a pair of ghosts. We stepped aside. The peacock chased him out through the door.

'You did not imagine, did you, that a peacock would have built its nest—and that nest would contain its eggs—in the same spot where the treasure was buried?'

Feluda's voice sounded as cold as steel. His revolver was pointed at Dr Hajra. It was clear to me now that the real culprit in this whole affair was Dr Hajra—and he had been suitably punished already—but there were so many other things that still seemed hazy that my head started reeling.

Then we heard a car.

Dr Hajra fell to the ground. He was lying on his stomach. He lifted his head and turned it slowly towards Feluda. His left hand, clutching a bloodstained handkerchief, was still pressed against his wound.

'There is absolutely no hope left for you. I hope you realize that? Every route of escape is closed, and...'

Before Feluda could finish speaking, Dr Hajra sprang to his feet and began running blindly in the opposite direction, away from the derelict house. Feluda lowered his gun because there really was no way that Dr Hajra could now escape. Two men, whom I recognized, were walking towards us. The one who was not hampered by a stick caught Dr Hajra neatly in his arms, as if he were a cricket ball.

The other man clutching the stick approached Feluda. I saw Feluda transfer his revolver to his left hand and offer the man his right hand. 'Hello, Dr Hajra!' he said.

What! That man was Dr Hajra?

He shook hands with Feluda. 'And you are Pradosh Mitter?'

'Yes. Those new naagras caused blisters on your feet, didn't they? Are they still bothering you?'

The real Dr Hajra smiled. 'I rang Mr Dhar the day before yesterday. He told me you were here. I had no problem in recognizing you from his description. Allow me to introduce you—this is Inspector Rathor.'

'And what about him?' Feluda pointed at the other man, whom until now we had known as Dr Hajra. He was now handcuffed and hanging his head, 'Is that Bhavananda?'

'Yes,' Dr Hajra replied, 'alias Amiyanath Burmun, alias the Great Bar-man—Wizard of the East!'

TWELVE

Bhavananda was handed over to the local police. The charges against him were many. They included an attempt to murder Hemanga Hajra, disappearing with his belongings, and trying to pass himself off as Dr Hajra.

We were back in the dak bungalow, having coffee (made with camel's milk) on the veranda. Mukul was romping happily on the lawn in front of us. He knew he would leave for Calcutta the same night. Having seen the golden fortress, he had no wish to remain in Rajasthan any longer.

Feluda turned to the real Dr Hajra and said, 'Bhavananda was truly a fraud, wasn't he? I mean, what he did in Chicago, and all that I read in the press reports...was all of it true?'

'Yes. One hundred per cent. Bhavananda and his accomplice cheated and swindled others in various countries, not just one. Besides, back in Chicago, they were doing something else. Not only were they out to deceive everyone, but they were also spreading evil tales and rumours about me, which was affecting my work. So, in the end, I was forced to take certain steps. But all that happened four years ago. I do not know when they returned to India. I came back only three months ago. One day, I happened to be in Mr Dhar's shop, when I heard about his son. So I went to meet him. You know the rest. When I decided to travel to Rajasthan with Mukul, I had no idea I'd be followed!'

'Who wouldn't want to kill two birds with one stone?' Feluda asked. 'There was the chance to grab that hidden treasure, plus settle scores with you...But didn't you see them anywhere in Calcutta?'

'No, not once. The first time I met them was in the refreshment room in the station at Bandikui. The two men came up to me and began chatting.'

'You didn't recognize them?'

'No, how could I? I had only seen them in Chicago, where they had long hair, flowing beards and fat moustaches!'

'What happened next?'

'They sat at the same table and had a meal with us. They told Mukul they knew magic and even pulled some tricks. Then they got into the same compartment with us. I got off at Kisangarh to show Mukul the fort there, but didn't realize that those two characters had followed me. They reached the fort soon after us, and hid somewhere until the coast was clear. It was a deserted place, in any case. There was no one in sight. When they found an opportunity, they pushed me down a slope. I rolled down, perhaps a hundred feet. Luckily, my fall was broken by a clump of bushes. If I take my shirt off, you'll see that my body is still covered with bruises. Anyway, I remained by the side of that bush for a whole hour. I wanted them to think that they had managed to get rid of me, and leave with Mukul. At least, Mukul would then be safe. By the time I got up and walked to the station, the eight o'clock train to Marwar had gone. Those two criminals had left by the same train, with Mukul and my luggage. All my papers were in my suitcase, so there was no way I could prove to anyone who I really was.'

'Didn't Mukul mind going with them?'

Dr Hajra smiled. 'Mukul was in a totally distracted state of mind. Didn't you realize that? He had no problem leaving his own parents and setting off with me. So why should he make a distinction between one strange man and another? Bhavananda told him he would take him to the golden fortress. That was enough to entice Mukul. Anyway, I didn't give up. If anything, I was more determined now to get to the bottom of this business. Fortunately, I still had my wallet with me. So I could buy new clothes—local Rajasthani ones. I packed my old torn ones into a bundle. I wasn't used to wearing naagras, you see, so I got blisters on my feet.

'The next day, I boarded the train at Kisangarh and got into your compartment. Then I took the same train as you from Marwar to Jodhpur. I went to stay in a place called Raghunath Sarai. I knew someone in Jodhpur—one Professor Trivedi. But, at first, I told him nothing. If the matter came to be known, the two men might have tried to run away, or Mukul himself might have felt scared and refused to cooperate. By then I had guessed that the fort in Jaisalmer was where Mukul should be taken. All I had to do was wait until Bhavananda had the same idea and left with Mukul. Until then, my job was to keep an eye on the pair.'

'We saw someone hanging around the Circuit House on the very first day. It was you, wasn't it?'

'Yes, and that caused another problem. Mukul saw me, and seemed to recognize me! At least, that's how it appeared from the way he came out of the gate and began walking straight towards me.'

'So, later, you followed Bhavananda and got into the same train that was going to Pokhran?'

'Yes. The strangest thing was that I saw you from the train, trying to stop it!'

'Bhavananda must have seen me, too. He would then have realized we would try to catch the early morning train from Ramdeora.'

Dr Hajra continued with his story. 'Before I caught that train, I told Trivedi to inform the police in Jaisalmer. Before that, I had spoken to Mr Dhar from Trivedi's house; and then I borrowed one of his suits to dress normally.'

'And when you got to Pokhran, you saw that Bhavananda's assistant was already there with a taxi, is that right?' Feluda wanted to know.

'That's where things went wrong. I lost them. Then I had to wait another ten hours and catch that early morning train. I had no idea that you were on the same train. I saw you here in the dak bungalow. Now, what I would like to know is, when did you first start suspecting Bhavananda?'

Feluda smiled. 'It would be wrong to say that I suspected Bhavananda. It was the character of Dr Hajra that made me suspicious. Not in Jodhpur, but in Bikaner. When we went to Devikund, we found him with his hands tied, his mouth gagged. Just before that, I'd found a matchbox with an ace printed on it. I knew that particular brand isn't sold in Rajasthan. Then, when we saw Dr Hajra lying on the ground so helplessly, at first I thought that matchbox was dropped by whoever had attacked him. But then I noticed that there was something wrong with the way he was tied up. I mean, if a man's hands and legs are tied, that may make him perfectly immobile; but if only his hands are tied behind his back, any intelligent man will fold his legs, slip his hands below them and loosen his ties. Then he can set himself free. It became clear to me that Dr Hajra had tied himself up. But even so, it did not occur to me at the time that that man was not the real Dr Hajra. The scales fell from my eyes this morning, in the train to Jaisalmer, when I happened to be staring at a note Bhavananda had written to me. He had used a sheet of your letterhead.'

'So? How was that significant?'

'The printed name showed "Hajra" with a "j". But Bhavananda, pretending to be you, had signed his name "Hazra", with a "z". That told me that the man I had met in Jodhpur and who had written that note was not the real Dr Hajra. But in that case, who was he? He had to be one of those men who had kidnapped Neelu. And the other man was Mandar Bose, who had one long nail on his right hand, who smoked cigars—Neelu had recognized the smell, and so had we. The question now was, who was the real Dr Hajra, and where was he? There could be only one answer to that—Hajra had to be that same man who had got into our compartment at Kisangarh, who had new naagras and blisters on his feet, who was seen loitering outside the Circuit House and the Bikaner fort, and who we saw this morning in the dak bungalow in Jaisalmer, limping with a stick in his hand!'

Dr Hajra nodded. 'Mr Dhar did a most intelligent thing by asking you to come here. I don't think I could have managed entirely on my own. It was you who tackled Bhavananda's assistant. If he is arrested as well, we can then say that it all ended happily.'

Feluda pointed at Lalmohan Babu and said, 'He made a significant contribution towards raising the alarm against Mandar Bose.'

Lalmohan Babu was struggling all this while to get in a word. Now he blurted out, 'I say, what's going to happen to that hidden treasure?'

'Why don't you leave it to the peacock?' said Dr Hajra. 'It's guarding it quite admirably, isn't it? You saw what happens when you meddle with a peacock!'

'For the moment,' suggested Feluda, 'kindly return the treasure you have got hidden. Mind you, from the way your jacket is bulging near your waist, one can hardly call it "hidden"!'

Lalmohan Babu looked positively sad as he pulled out Mandar Bose's revolver and returned it to Feluda.

'Thank you,' said Feluda as he took it. Then his face suddenly grew grave. I saw him examine the revolver closely.

'I must hand it to you, Mr Trotter!' he muttered. 'Who knew you'd hoodwink Pradosh Mitter like this?'

'Why, what's happened?' we cried.

'This revolver's a fake! Made in Japan. Magicians use such guns on the stage!'

Just before everyone burst into laughter, Lalmohan Babu took the revolver back from Feluda, grinned and said, 'For my collection—and as a souvenir of our powerful adventure in Rajasthan. Thank you, sir!'

২০ নং ছবি

সোনার কেল্লা

সত্যজিৎ রায়

II. THE FILM

SONAR KELLA

Produced by the Government of West Bengal, Ray's twentieth feature film *Sonar Kella* (*The Golden Fortress*) was released on 27 December 1974.

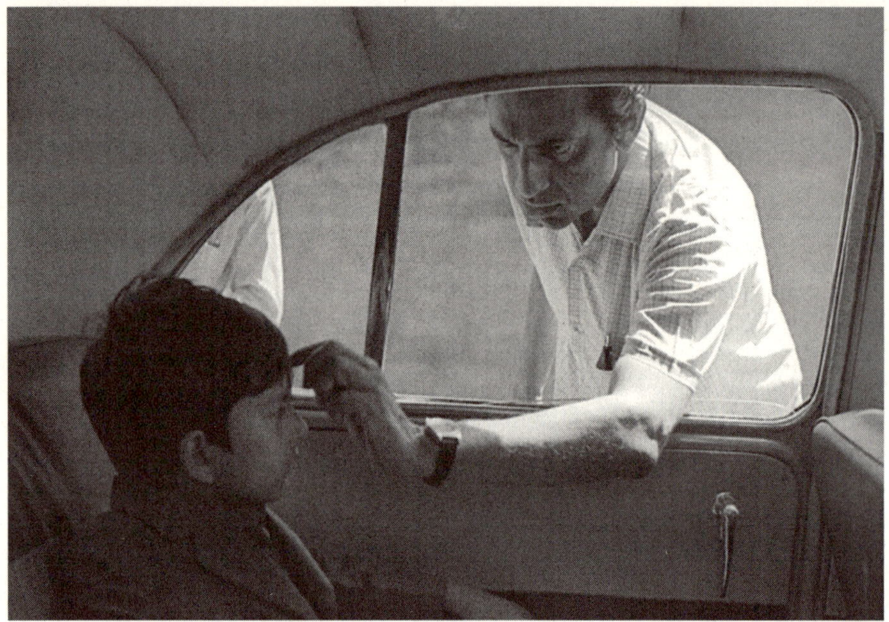

Behind the scenes with Kushal Chakraborty, who played Mukul in the film. Photograph by Sandip Ray

Giving last minute touch to the make-up of 'Jatayu' Santosh Dutta. Photograph by Sandip Ray

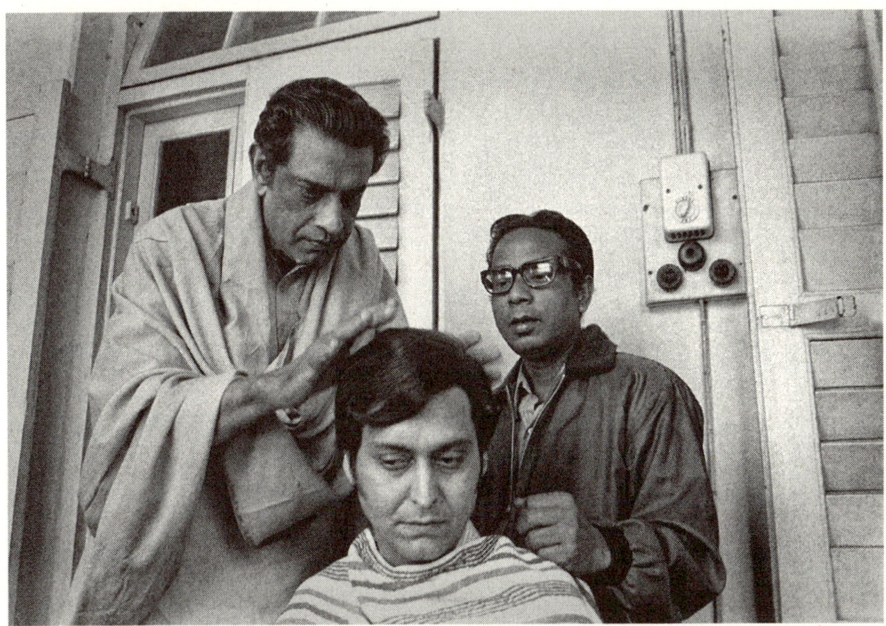

Ray and Soumitra form a formidable pair as seen in the camaraderie shared by them. Photograph by Sandip Ray

The director in action on location in Rajasthan. Photograph by Sandip Ray

Ray in discussion with Santosh Dutta on location in Lathi station, Rajasthan. Photograph by Tarapada Banerjee

FILM SYNOPSIS

Ray deviated from the whodunnit format and adopted a different narrative for the screenplay of the film. This synopsis, written by Ray is sourced from his *kheror khata* and is previously unpublished.

Mukul, the seven-year-old son of Sudhir Dhar, a bookseller, suddenly begins to show signs of remembering a pervious birth in a region where there was a Golden Fortress. He also talks of having seen battles, peacocks, camels and so on.

A parapsychologist called Dr Hajra, who is doing research on rebirth, examines Mukul and comes to the conclusion that the boy must be talking of western Rajasthan. Sudhir agrees to let the parapsychologist take Mukul to Jodhpur where Dr Hajra hopes to find the boy's place of previous birth and the Golden Fortress.

One day before Mukul's departure for Rajasthan, he is interviewed by a journalist whom the boy tells of having seen precious stones. The journalist turns this into a 'buried treasure' story, which comes out in the papers the next day.

Two crooks, Mandar and Burman, a magician and a hypnotist, read the story, and decide to kidnap Mukul and find out about the buried treasure. They kidnap another boy by mistake from the same neighbourhood, learn from him that Mukul has gone to Jodhpur, return the boy and leave for Jodhpur.

Mukul's father hears of the kidnapping and, anxious for Mukul's safety, comes to the detective Felu Mitter. Felu decides to go to Jodhpur to protect Dr Hajra and Mukul. In the meantime, after a day's halt at Agra, Dr Hajra and Mukul board the same train that contains the two crooks—Mandar and Burman. When the crooks learn of this, they decide to get rid of Dr Hajra and take the boy with them. Next morning Hajra is pushed off a precipice by Mandar in Kishangarh while visiting the fort there with Mukul. Mandar and Burman, in the meantime, strike up a friendship with the boy. The three continue on their journey to Jodhpur.

Hajra recovers, having escaped death by being miraculously caught in a bush halfway down the hillside. Badly injured, he staggers into Kishangarh town and is treated by a sympathetic doctor.

In the meantime, Felu and his fourteen-year-old cousin Topshe are on their way to Jodhpur. During their journey they make the acquaintance of Lalmohan Ganguly—a popular writer of thrillers. Felu doesn't reveal that he is a professional detective engaged in the pursuit of criminals. At Kishangarh, Dr Hajra enters the compartment dressed in Rajasthani costumes. Felu notices the signs of injury and realizes there is something mysterious about this character, but he doesn't realize that this is the man he is supposed to meet in Jodhpur and help.

Felu and Topshe arrive at the Circuit House in Jodhpur. Burman is now impersonating Dr Hajra and Mandar is supposedly a globe trotter. Felu introduces himself to Burman, who realizes that his task has now become complicated by the presence of a detective. Mandar and Burman decide that they have to get rid of Felu at the earliest opportunity.

The real Hajra is now in Jodhpur, and is looking for an opportunity to take his revenge on the crooks and rescue the boy from their clutches.

Mukul has, in the meantime, rejected several forts, and when a trip to Bikaner also proves to be futile, Burman—now anxious to achieve his end quickly—decides to try hypnotism to make him remember the name of his place of birth.

Felu, in the meantime, has become suspicious of Mandar, but still doesn't suspect Burman, who has been playing the role of Dr Hajra quite convincingly.

That night, Burman manages to hypnotize Mukul, and in that state the boy reveals the name of the place. It is Jaisalmer.

The next day is supposed to be a day of rest. In the morning, while Felu goes exploring in the bazaar, Burman discretely goes off to the station to catch the morning train to

Pokhran. Mandar is left behind to deal with Felu. The plan is to tell Felu that Mukul has suddenly remembered the place of his birth—Barmer—and Dr Hajra has gone with the boy, and Felu should follow him.

In the bazaar, Felu suddenly comes upon some stoneware made in Jaisalmer. The golden yellow colour immediately signals to him that Jaisalmer must be the place with the Golden Fortress. He rushes to the Circuit House to report to Dr Hajra but finds that they have left for Barmer. He is puzzled to learn from Mandar that Mukul mentioned Barmer as his place of birth.

At this point, Felu's attention is accidentally caught by a visiting card of the real Dr Hajra. The name is spelt H-A-J-R-A. Felu rushes to the reception, and, looking in the register, finds that Hajra has been spelt with a Z. Felu realizes the boy has gone off with an imposter.

He decides to take a chance and go to Jaisalmer. Mandar is greatly upset by Felu's decision. He was supposed to go to Pokhran by taxi, collect Barman and the boy and go to Jaisalmer.

He now sets off, and on the way he puts broken pieces of glass on the road to fail Felu's attempt to reach Jaisalmer.

Felu sets off with Topshe and Lalmohan. The car's tyre bursts in two places, thanks to Mandar, and Felu has to finally resort to camels.

They reach Ramdeora where they can catch the midnight train to Jaisalmer. At the station Mandar is waiting in disguise for an opportunity to finish off Felu. The train arrives (the same train is carrying the real Dr Hajra to Jaisalmer—still looking for the boy). Mandar's attempt to kill Felu fails. In fact, he is submitted to the mercy of Felu, but manages to escape at the last moment—only to get into the compartment that contains the man he thought he had killed. The encounter with Dr Hajra is too much for Mandar—who is slightly drunk—and he falls off the train in an attempt to back away from the 'ghost'.

In Jaisalmer, Burman takes Mukul to his village of birth, and is anxious to find out the location of his house so that he can go for the buried treasure. Approaching the house, Burman is suddenly confronted by peacocks. As a child, Burman had been bitten by a peacock, and he has a phobia of the bird.

Burman tries to shoo off the birds, and finally has to bring out his revolver. This upsets Mukul, and he now turns violently against Burman, running away from him.

Burman pursues the boy desperately but is again and again foiled by peacocks getting in his way.

In the meantime, Felu and company arrive and Burman has to surrender.

Mukul now recovers his normalcy, realizes he is amongst friends again. He is asked where he wants to go, and he says, 'Back home in Calcutta.'

CAMEL VERSUS TRAIN

The piece, written in Bengali by Ray documents the experience of shooting in Rajasthan.

First published in *Sandesh* Summer Number 1975.

Translated by Bijaya Ray

Those who have seen the film *Sonar Kella* (*The Golden Fortress*) will know that there is a rather interesting episode in it involving camels. The writer of crime thrillers, Lalmohan Ganguli alias Jatayu, has often dreamt of riding a camel in the desert. Towards the end of the film his dream comes true in an extraordinary manner. The villain, Mandar Bose, who is being pursued by Feluda, manages to ensure that the detective's car gets a puncture, not once but twice, thus foiling his plans to get to Jaisalmer by road. Stranded in the middle of nowhere, Feluda and his companions spot a group of Rajasthani men riding camels. Feluda decides to take a lift on those camels to the nearest railway station which is at Ramdeora, eight miles away. They can then catch the train to Jaisalmer which calls at Ramdeora at midnight.

Feluda and Topshe have nothing to worry about. Both are young, smart and used to regular exercise. But Jatayu? Faced with camels in real life, his dream quickly turns into a nightmare. What strange animals they are! Dim and droopy eyes like drug addicts, large, uneven teeth, chewing some mysterious object all day long. And when they move, they sway so much that it seems as if every bone in the body of the rider would come apart. If he has to climb one of these creatures, heaven knows what misfortunes might lie in store. But there is nothing Jatayu can do. Feluda and Topshe spring up on the camel's back with no problem. Lalmohan Babu tries, nearly loses his balance, but somehow manages to hang on. 'Chaliye ji, Ramdeora!' Feluda says to the leader of the group.

As they start moving, with Lalmohan Babu still feeling terrified, Topshe suddenly sees a train in the distance. If the train can be stopped, they can save themselves a ten-hour wait at Ramdeora. The camels start running towards the train and soon reach the railway line. Feluda takes out a white handkerchief from his pocket and starts waving it anxiously, in the hope that the driver will see him and stop the train. But that does not happen. The driver ignores him completely, and the train simply whooshes past, whistling loudly. Feluda grits his teeth and says, 'Shabaash!' By this time, Jatayu is half dead. This is an experience he is never going to forget. The group makes an about turn and resume their journey to Ramdeora.

This, basically, was the sequence that had to be shot. Now, if I describe the problems we had to face to shoot just these few scenes, you will get an idea of what an elaborate process film-making is.

***

Everyone knows there is no dearth of camels in Rajasthan. While making *Goopy Gyne Bagha Byne*, we had to get hold of one thousand camels in just two or three days. For *Sonar Kella*, our need was much less. But the problem was that the place we had selected was far removed from any kind of habitation. As far as the eye could see, there was only an expanse of sand, dotted with thorny bushes and dried grass. A meter gauge line cut across the desert, seemingly without a beginning or an end. A motorway to Jaisalmer ran parallel to the railway track. Had it been further away, we could not have shot a single scene here. We were based in Jaisalmer and our crew had to bring all our luggage to this chosen spot. The cameraman had to get into an open-topped jeep with the camera in order to catch the camels running towards the train. It was essential therefore to have a paved road nearby.

We had to travel the hundred miles from Jodhpur to Jaisalmer and search every inch of the way before we found this place which seemed most suitable. It was about seventy miles to the east of Jaisalmer, in the direction of Jodhpur. The camels had to be brought from a village called Khachi, seven miles further east. The owners of the camels were told to dress them well. We may well laugh at the appearance of a camel, but to a Rajasthani, a camel is his best friend, sometimes the only thing that can keep him alive in the desert. So, from ancient times, they have shown this animal a lot of affection by dressing it in colourful embroidered sheets, tassels, and even jewellery. When they move in a row across the desert, in all their finery, they seem to merge beautifully with the harsh and dry landscape. No other animal would have fitted in as well into the desert landscape as these ones. The owners said they would reach the spot by afternoon. It was agreed that some of our men would wait for them there, or they would find it impossible to locate the exact area.

We had got the camels, now we had to get a train. The one we had decided to use ran in the morning from Jodhpur to Pokhran. Pokhran was between Jodhpur and Jaisalmer. The exact spot where the shooting was to take place was twenty miles to the west of Pokhran, but we were more or less confident that the authorities would allow us to take the train where we needed it.

***

As we were getting ready for the big day, something happened that nearly destroyed all our plans. Suddenly, the price of coal went up, and the train we were going to use was cancelled at a day's notice. What a disaster! I had written this particular scene so carefully. Were we now going to have to drop the idea of showing Feluda and his team running through the desert on camels, trying to stop a train? No, we could not allow that to happen.

I met the railway authorities the same day, and explained that if this scene could not be shot, the main purpose of our visit to Rajasthan was going to be defeated. Fortunately, some of the officials I spoke to were sympathetic. They understood our problem and found a solution. They offered to give us a whole train, complete with six carriages, the guard's cabin, a coal tender and, of course, an engine. All we had to do was pay for the coal used. Oh, what a relief it was to see this problem so easily solved! In fact, it turned out to be a blessing in disguise for now the train was entirely at our disposal, at least for a few hours. We could make it start and stop, or run backwards and forwards, just as we liked.

It was decided that the train would wait for us at Pokhran. We would travel to Pokhran from Jaisalmer (a matter of a hundred miles) by car and board the train which would then leave for the spot in the desert where Feluda, Topshe and Jatayu would be waiting for us. On our way to this spot, we would take a few shots of Mukul (the little boy who wants to see the golden fortress) and the second villain called Barman (who has kidnapped Mukul, assisted by Mandar Bose). The scene would show the two inside the train — Barman nodding off, and Mukul staring out of the window, deeply engrossed in the scenery.

There was something else I wanted to show in my film. If I could get inside the coal tender, I could take a shot of the engine. It would be quite easy to get a close up of the engine's chimney, ejecting thick black smoke. Through this smoke, I could show the two railway lines running parallel to each other, stretching right up to the horizon.

The first hitch occurred at Pokhran. The train that was supposed to arrive at half past eleven, turned up at half past two. A delay of three hours meant complete chaos, especially when even a short delay of fifteen minutes could throw our carefully planned schedule out of gear. However, there was no point in wasting any more time arguing, so we picked up our luggage and got into the train.

The few shots with Mukul and Barman went off quite smoothly. Then the train was stopped so that I could get into the coal tender with two of my assistants. There was nothing here except a great mound of coal. I stood on this mound, camera in hand, and told the driver to start the train. He had a companion, who was the stoker. His job was to pick up pieces of coal with a huge shovel, and load them into the boiler. This kept the fire going which, in turn, helped a steady column of smoke hiss out of the chimney.

I stood on the mound of coal, my elbows pressed against the roof of the engine for support. In my hand I held the camera. As I was peering through it, my feet slipped now and then and I kept losing my balance. At first, I was greatly puzzled by this; but when I had finished taking the final shot, I realized that because I had been standing right on top of the mound the poor stoker had had no choice but to dig the coal from under my feet. Now I could fully understand the true meaning of the saying 'the rug was pulled from under my feet' !

We reached the site for the shooting to find the actors and the remaining crew waiting anxiously. The only thing that had failed to wait for us was the sun. It had started to set already. By the time we got the camera ready, it would undoubtedly disappear completely. There was no way we could shoot this precious scene in the fading light. There was nothing we could do, except pack up and go back home. But it was agreed that the following day, we would all return to the same spot at half past two, including the camels. The train would also arrive here without stopping at Pokhran.

***

As I have mentioned already, we were based at Jaisalmer. About half a mile from the famous golden fortress, we had found a small palace that was now being used as a guest house.

It was large enough to accommodate the whole unit, which had nearly thirty-five people. The next morning, we rose early and went straight into the fort to shoot the last few scenes of the film. Then we returned to the guest house for a quick lunch, before going back to the same spot as the day before. We got there by half past two to find that the camels and their owners had already arrived. Now we only had to wait for the train to turn up. One look at the sky told me that the postponement of our shooting was another blessing in disguise. The sky was now flecked with grey and white clouds. Golden sunlight, streaming through the gaps in the clouds fell on the desert, thereby giving us a light that was suitably striking for this dramatic scene.

The train, too, arrived most punctually. We could not, of course, help feeling anxious until it did, for we all knew that this was our last chance to shoot the scene. It was essential for us to return to Jodhpur the next day to leave Rajasthan and go back to Calcutta in the evening. When at last we heard the train huffing and puffing on its way, a collective sigh of relief went up from the entire unit.

The driver saw us and stopped the train. We then explained what was required of him. He would have to go back a quarter of a mile. Then he would have to come forward again to meet us. We would start our camera as soon as the train came into view, and get the camels to start running with Feluda and team on their back. The open-topped jeep would wait on the road with the camera in it, and move alongside the camels.

The driver seemed to understand everything, except what had not actually been spelt out. As a result of this, our first attempt to take the shot failed rather miserably. As the train got closer, the camels began their run, and with them ran our jeep. Then they reached the railway line and Feluda took out his handkerchief to wave at the driver. With a squeal of the brakes, the train stopped almost at once. 'Why did you stop?' we asked the driver. 'Why,' he replied innocently, 'that Babu just waved his hanky and asked me to stop, didn't he?' The poor driver did not know the story of the film, so obviously had no idea what a difference his action would make to the following events. Anyway, we had to get ready for take two. Train, go back. Camels, go back. Jeep, go back. Start again. This time, everyone knew what had to be done. There should not be any problem.

The train reversed for a quarter of a mile and started again. There it was...we could hear it coming...it was almost within view...camels, get ready. A group of men were about to start pushing the jeep. The first attempt had made them break into a sweat. They were bracing themselves for the second.

I opened my mouth to say, 'Start camera!' but the words froze on my lips. The train was coming, yes, but where was the smoke? The whole idea was to show the glowing desert landscape disappear momentarily behind a thick layer of smoke from the engine. How else would the scene be interesting and exciting? Stop, stop, stop again...train, camels, jeep. We had to start all over again.

Every member of the unit left their position and rushed forward to stop the train, their arms raised high. *Roko, roko*!

The train squealed to a stop once more.

What had happened to the smoke? The stoker made a confession. He was so busy watching the shooting that he had forgotten to put enough coal in the boiler. No wonder there was no smoke. Okay, but this time we could not afford another mistake. The light was just right. If we had to make a fourth attempt, it would be gone. I decided not to take any chances, and got one of our own men to join the stoker.

Feluda, Topshe and Jatayu mounted their camels once more. There was one advantage in taking the same shot three times. I knew none of the actors would have to pretend to be tired and uncomfortable. Jatayu already looked as if all he wanted to do was go home. Nevertheless, each of them wanted the shot to be perfect, so they were all prepared to ignore their personal discomfort.

Luckily, everything went according to plan the third time. We ended up with a shot that was perfect in every way.

However, this did not mean that our work was over. We still needed the train later that night at ten o'clock, to shoot another scene showing the railway station at Ramdeora. The train to Jaisalmer would arrive in the middle of the night, and Feluda, Topshe and Lalmohan would get into it. As the train started to move, Mandar Bose, dressed as a Rajasthani, would run and grab the handle of their compartment.

But that is another story.

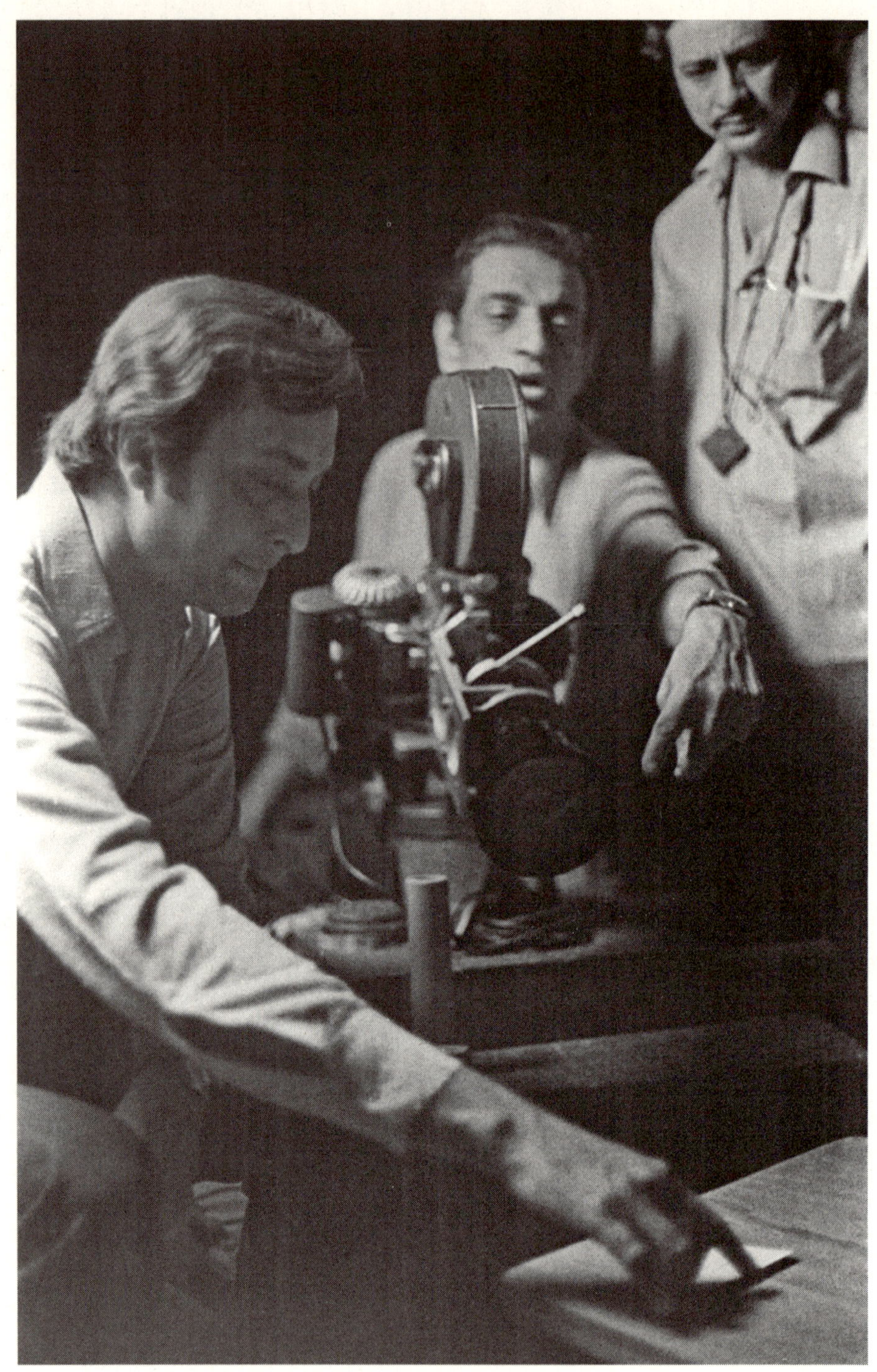

Ray giving instructions to Soumitra Chatterjee as Soumendu Roy looks on. Photograph by Sandip Ray

FUN, CAMELS AND GREED CONTROL

Extracted from *Master and I* by Soumitra Chatterjee

Translated by Arunava Sinha

After *Ashani Sanket* all of us began work on the wonderfully joyous film *Sonar Kella*. Manik-da (Ray was fondly called by his pet name 'Manik') informed me that I would have to play Felu, a character in a series of detective stories that he had himself written.

As far as I can recollect, Felu-da was introduced to the world when the children's magazine *Sandesh* was relaunched in its new phase. Felu Mittir and his team made their appearance in Manik-da's imagination when he sat down to write for the magazine. Like everyone else, I too read the stories eagerly when they were published. I had liked *Badshahi Angti* (*The Royal Ring*), the first mystery novel featuring Felu-da, very much indeed. I particularly enjoyed the business of flinging chilli powder in the adversary's eyes and escaping towards the end of the novel. There were many discussions over *Badshahi Angti*, but Manik-da had probably not yet thought of making a film with a Felu story.

However, since Manik-da didn't say anything specifically, I cannot be certain whether he had thought of filming Felu at this stage. But I had, and I kept thinking about it. The reason for this was the intrinsic appeal of the Felu stories. The story was so well laid out, the settings and twists and turns (all following the logic of the narrative), the different characters and their dialogue were all so perfect that it felt as though the writer had consciously set the process of writing the screenplay into motion—all that was left was to actually write it. Even the travels were presented so alluringly that the reader and his suitcase seemed to join Topshe, Lalmohanbabu and Felu Mittir on their journeys.

In addition to Felu's behaviour and gestures, what I tried to remember constantly was that Felu was a thinking man. I simply couldn't afford to forget his cerebral ways. A sharply intelligent person is trying to use incisive analysis to solve a mystery—I was conscious of the fact that my expression had to bring this out. I had attempted to maintain a continuity of this expression right through the film. I had specifically thought of using my eyes, eyebrows and a frown. An intelligent person's glance grow sharper when needed. Perhaps there are clever people who can conceal this—I cannot say. I believe that in certain situations a pair of bright, lively (at times restless) and articulate eyes signal that deep thoughts are running through the mind. This was what I had tried to use in Felu's case, and Manik-da had not objected. Audiences and Manik-da would have judged how successful I was—I cannot comment on this.

In this context I am reminded of a specific scene in *Sonar Kella*, where Felu accepts Dr Hazra's card, whereupon thoughts of whether the doctor spelt his name with a 'j' or a 'z' begin to crowd his mind. I am sitting in a low chair, the card lying on a table in front of me. I am thinking with my hand on my brow, the position of the hand signalling that I was analysing things. When you're working with an extraordinary director, even a tiny instruction at a critical juncture can transform the very dimension of the performance. Rehearsals were underway when Manik-da slipped in an instruction—'At this point drum your fingers on your forehead, Soumitra, as though you're playing a musical instrument.' His instruction flashed like a bolt of lightning in my head and Felu's expression acquired an extra dimension. There's also an instance of the use of the eyes in a scene that takes place soon after this one, with a worried Felu pacing up and down while the camera follows him.

Santosh-da's performance as Jatayu will remain an immortal asset of Bengali cinema. When Sandip Roy later made TV films in Hindi with the Felu stories, I discussed this with Manik-da. After we had watched the first episode, he said, 'No, without you and Santosh, Bengalis will not take this well. They won't accept this version.'

There are probably very few detective stories featuring a jovial real-life writer of detective stories. Jatayu's manner of speaking was a source of enjoyment to everyone, from young boys and girls to old men and women. Jatayu was constantly in search of the title of his next thriller. His anxious conversation always included Hindi and English words, pronounced in his unique way. When agitated, he used portmanteau words in his haste, such as 'hyanes', combing the Bangla 'hyan' with the English 'yes'. Only he could have asked a question like *'Kanta ki era bechhe khaaye?'* when told that camels primarily eat 'kantagaachh' or thorny cactus plants. Felu, even Topshe, frequently correct the innumerable mistakes that Lalmohan-babu makes. But the ability to spring a surprise is not one-way—once in a while Lalmohan-babu can even startle Felu Mittir, such as when he says, 'Did you know Rammohan Roy's grandson owned a circus?' Jatayu had this kind of dialogue too.

The unusual free-hand exercises that Manik-da depicted in *Sonar Kella* had to be shown in the interest of the film, but in real life Santosh-da was an extremely fit man, who exercised regularly—which was quite natural for a professional actor. Santosh-da was usually in very good health, with fitness levels matching those of athletes of his age. Let me inform those who can recollect the scene shot at Lathi station that the manner in which Santosh-da stretched his limbs was an indirect display of his physical fitness. Making such funny movements smoothly is impossible unless one exercises regularly. None of us had ever ridden on the back of a camel before we shot for *Sonar Kella*. The rhythmic gait of the camel was not familiar to us, and it was true that the undulating movements of its body were new as well. But whatever little apprehension we might have felt was far outweighed by the fun of it all. That Lalmohan-babu appeared close to tears was nothing but a reflection of Manik-da's grip on reality and Santosh-da's acting prowess.

Besides the older characters, there were several young people in *Sonar Kella* too, with Mukul being one of the principal figures. The role of Mukul was played by master Kushal Chakraborty. A very clever and lively boy, whose company all of us enjoyed. Let's say we were returning to the hotel after a day's work, barely able to drag ourselves along in fatigue. But master Kushal was bursting with curiosity about everything—the variety of his questions was endless. We answered some of his queries, responding to the rest with, 'Later, OK?' and so on. But it was different with Manik-da, for he was a genuine friend of children.

Many people have been curious about the effectiveness with which Manik-da could extract wonderful performances from children and young actors. There was only one secret to this—he never thought of children as children, giving them as much importance as adults, and mingling with them as though he was one of them.

As a result they were quick to make friends with him. Being in the company of the director Satyajit Ray, a man of extraordinary taste, offered constant opportunities for learning. Take the time we were driving through the extensive desert, in the scene where Mandar Bose has left shards of glass on the road to prevent Felu Mittir & Co. from progressing further. Manik-da shot a beautiful scene at the spot where the car tyre was punctured, but it was left out of the film eventually. He had shot it with great care, including the sand, cactus and sunlight on the desert—a conversation between Felu, Topshe and Jatayu while the punctured tyre is being repaired.

But later, when the scene seemed unnecessary to the demands of the screenplay, Manik-da cut it out ruthlessly on the editing table. I was extremely surprised at this. Manik-da used to regard his art with incredible attention and integrity. It didn't take him a moment to leave out such a wonderful scene simply because he felt it was unnecessary, like flab on the screenplay. This was a very valuable lesson—how to control your greed as a director.

A VOYAGE IN INDIA

Excerpts from an interview with Satyajit Ray by John Hughes

Film Comment, 12(4) Sept–Oct 1976

A recent Ray film, *The Golden Fortress*, does journey into a strange old world of artifice only to situate us even more firmly in the contemporary realities of India. In the manner of John Ford, Ray wanted to make a 'light film' to counterbalance the 'seriousness' of *Distant Thunder*. *The Golden Fortress* was designed for the youth audience in India, but the result is a rather bizarre, phantasmagorical romance with the erotic overtones of some of the less explicit Indian temple structures. A young boy in Calcutta gets into the newspapers because of his ability to describe in amazing detail the treasure-filled medieval fortress where he lives in previous incarnation. He is kidnapped and taken on a tour of the extant fortresses by a pair of vicious yet hilarious Truffaut-like crooks, who are tracked down by a lethargic detective (Soumitra Chatterjee) accompanied by a young assistant and, during the latter part of the film, by a bumbling writer of detective and mystery novels. The Golden Fortress is discovered, and the boy is rescued from both the bandits and his final empty despair.

I saw the film recently at Columbia University's Bengali Student Club, where I also managed to penetrate a bee swarm of Indian journalists in order to meet Satyajit Ray. Amid the delighted and delightful Bengalis watching the film, I suddenly felt that the mystery of the golden fortress, however sublime, was something tangible that could be incorporated forever into one's life. The impression was momentary, but I attempted to maintain it by visiting Ray the next day at the St Regis. Ray was gently hospitable, although occasionally irritated by the flashing light on his telephone. After several minutes of talk I finally remembered to turn on the tape recorder.

SATYAJIT RAY: The gangsters in *The Golden Fortress* are a bit different from those we got to know in American films. They're not nearly so fierce or so sinister. They're rather bumbling types.

JOHN HUGHES: The elliptical montage with which you introduce them reminded me of Truffaut's take-off on the comic aspects of the American gangster figure in *Shoot the Piano Player*.

SATYAJIT RAY: There is some of that take off quality in the film, I think. And I wanted to make a mild film. It was aimed at the younger element in my audience, although everyone went to see it, regardless of age. The young have responded very well to my recent series of children's books, of which *The Golden Fortress* is a part, and they especially seemed to like the detective figure with his fourteen-year-old cousin as a sort of Watson-like character. All seven books are written from the point of view of the child.

JOHN HUGHES: Were you interested in parapsychology when you wrote the book?

SATYAJIT RAY: I had met a parapsychologist who was doing research on children who had claimed to be reincarnations. Like the gangsters in the film, he would actually take them to locations described by the children as locales of their previous incarnations. 'There was a mountain, with a great river and a temple…' He would try to guess where it was, and then take them there to see if they recognized it!

JOHN HUGHES: *The Golden Fortress* is a lovely fantasy, but it has so many colour variations on your usual neo-realist style—the shots in Calcutta, on the desert, etc.—that it bothers me a bit to hear that you will make a big-budget film in Hindi in the near future. And in the studios of Bombay!

SATYAJIT RAY: You shouldn't be worried. It will be a very serious film on a very serious historical event. The background will be the year preceding the Indian mutiny of 1859. It takes place in a city in the region around Delhi, and it concerns two chess-playing friends, upper-class Moslems. It was a period of extreme decadence in that particular state. The king was a very fine poet, but a bad ruler. It was a very fertile area, and the about-to-retire Viceroy decided to annex the state and present it as a final gift to the queen. In his diaries he wrote: 'I'm going to pluck this ripe fruit and give it to Victoria…' So the film will be about this annexation, and how the two chess players try to save their own kings as the actual is captured. It's a story about non-involvement, about decadence, as well as a great many other things. Hindi will be used because that is the language spoken in this state. And it will also present me with a wider audience.

JOHN HUGHES: *The Golden Fortress* seems to me to be a very serious film also, despite the youth orientation. Like *Days and Nights in the Forest* it is a film about neo-colonialism in India today. And there is the same theme of a voyage to India, if I may paraphrase your friend Rossellini. Western-style gangsters journeying into the ancient heart of India…

SATYAJIT RAY: You can be sure that they had spent a lot of time looking at American movies! But *Days and Nights* is more a psychological voyage than a straight forward adventure story.

JOHN HUGHES: But the boy's crying within the fortress at the end is psychological.

SATYAJIT RAY: I don't think so. He feels very alone in this ancient town now that the gangster has been exposed by this strange detective and his friends who have just arrived on the scene. But then he laughs loudly, and that's a return to normality for the boy. He hasn't laughed throughout the film, ever since the photographer asked him to smile at the beginning. There was no reason for him to feel amused. The final laugh brings the film to a full conclusion.

JOHN HUGHES: But there is a movement towards a kind of mythopoeic truth in all of your recent films. The birdsong at the end of *The Adversary*, for example.

SATYAJIT RAY: But that's very iconic, of course. He has remembered the birdcall as taking place in a very sylvan setting, but he finally hears it again amidst the very drab surroundings of a small suburban town. The bird, obviously, doesn't choose its locations! It can just as easily appear in a setting of squalor. That's the irony of it, you see. But he has found the bird again, which gives us another rounded-off conclusion.

JOHN HUGHES: As in Charulata's poem writing where all of India flashes before her eyes. In *Charulata*, also, you have the theme of some mythopoeic truth hidden beneath the crust of neo-colonialism...

SATYAJIT RAY: Or of technology. The incursion of certain elements of 'civilization'.

JOHN HUGHES: I'm also thinking of the peacocks that guard the non-existent treasure at the end of *The Golden Fortress*.

SATYAJIT RAY: That's simply a bit of local colour. Peacocks are as numerous as crows in Calcutta and in that entire part of India. Also, I liked the idea that a bird could scare away an armed gangster, simply because the gangster remembered having been bitten by one as a child. In the original book I had the peacocks laying eggs around the treasure site in order to...but that's another story.

JOHN HUGHES: I still think it's a rather psychological ending.

SATYAJIT RAY: You were talking about Freud before the interview, and I certainly think that Freud as well Marx can't be ignored; they're the major influences on the last half of the twentieth century. I'm always very aware of psychological motivations, although I haven't studied Freud.

JOHN HUGHES: I was thinking of the golden bowls that give Soumitra Chatterjee, who plays the detective, his first real clue as to the location of the fortress.

SATYAJIT RAY: Yes, I see what you mean. By the way, Chatterjee was uncertain as to whether the public would accept him in the part of the detective, with no heroine around! He seemed to resemble the illustrations of the detective that I had done for the book. But he thought he might be overshadowed by the colourful writer-figure in the film, as well as by the colourful crooks. I told him: 'Your doing nothing will eventually emerge as the very spine of the film!' And his sombre personality did become a marvelous foil for the silly writer and the bumbling crooks.

JOHN HUGHES: You got fantastic comic performances from the crooks. Kamu Mukherji, who played the tall crook, was as funny as he was vicious. I liked the way he literally steps into his leather jacket to put it on.

SATYAJIT RAY: I've often observed him doing that. He's a very strange, amazing character. He comes to my house, quite often, and he's full of wonderful stories, magic tricks, and impersonations.

JOHN HUGHES: In *The Golden Fortress*, what is the role of the ancient fortresses and cities that the film explored in a fashion that reminds me of late Rossellini? Are they the real India, or just another kind of illusion?

SATYAJIT RAY: I haven't seen any of his recent films. Those palaces and fortresses are deserted now, they're protected monuments.

The crew shooting at the entrance of the Bikaner Fort. Photograph by Sandip Ray

JOHN HUGHES: They're scary, too…

SATYAJIT RAY: Of course, they're scary—but there is something glorious about them also. There was a planned city within Jaisalmer, the so called Golden Fortress that was studied by the architect Corbusier. The stone sculpture is extraordinary; they had a real sense of beauty. The streets are wide and paved with stone. Even in the most intense desert heat the interiors are perfectly cool.

JOHN HUGHES: Everyone knows of the influence of Renoir, Rossellini, Kurusawa, etc. on your work. But I was surprised to see so many traces of the American gangster film appearing in this supposed children's fantasy, *The Golden Fortress*.

SATYAJIT RAY: It is designed to reach that audience, who have loved my books but have little opportunity to see my 'serious' films. But there are other levels. Even earlier than Renoir and Rossellini were my connections with the American cinema. I enjoyed and appreciated many American films in the forties. I remember seeing Walsh, Hawks and Huston's *Beat the Devil*, which is a marvelous take-off on gangster films.

JOHN HUGHES: When the scorpion almost kills Chatterjee in *The Golden Fortress*, it reminded me of the scorpion in Nick Ray's *Bitter Victory*.

SATYAJIT RAY: I hadn't thought of that at all. I saw *Bitter Victory* in 1957, in Venice, where it was in competition with *Aparajito*, which won the award. Nicholas and I were afterwards on the jury at Berlin. People talked about the two Rays converging. The scorpion, again, is something you would find in that part of the country, in the dry, hot country.

JOHN HUGHES: You know the countryside well, and yet you're a city person.

SATYAJIT RAY: Yes, I am, but I love the countryside. As an advertising man I would go for excursions by train into the countryside to sketch or take photographs. I feel deeply rooted in Bengal and its traditions. I love the country bazaars and village fairs. The theme of childhood memories of the countryside, as you've pointed out, is important for me.

RAY ON SONAR KELLA

Excerpts from *Satyajit Ray's Art* by Firoze Rangoonwalla, Clarion Books, 1980

After this (*Ashani Sanket*) I decided again to make a film for young people. This time I based it on one of my own published stories. I have been writing these stories ever since I revived my children's magazine (*Sandesh*) in 1961. One of the things was a series of detective stories based on a character I had created like Sherlock Holmes and a young assistant like Watson, named Feluda and Topse. It was set in Jaisalmer in Rajasthan, an area I grew to love when I had shot *Goopy Gyne*. The story in fact grew out of my experience there. It is a mystery surrounding a little boy who claims to be reincarnation and talks of buried treasure. It was great fun making *Sonar Kella* and in colour because of the beauty of the setting.

It was quite an expensive production financed by West Bengal Government. I thought they would be interested in financing a film for children. I approached them and they agreed. The film was an immediate success. It has not been widely shown abroad. There have been offers for distribution there. But the Government is not equipped to handle this side of the business and it has not followed up the offers it has received by it so far. But I am sure this is also going to be shown abroad later. But I was very pleased with the success at home. If sub-titled or dubbed, it can also be a success in other parts of our country because now my stories are being translated into Hindi, Marathi, Gujarati and even Malayalam. In time the character of Feluda will be known to non-Bengali audiences also and there may be a fresh demand for this film.

REVIEW

Variety, New York 1975

With *The Golden Fortress*, India's top filmmaker, Satyajit Ray, shows exactly what kind of children's film can be made when a major talent is behind the helm—entertaining, non-patronizing fare that can beguile youngsters and oldsters alike. It's a kind of film that points out the glaring weaknesses in films being turned out recently by some major studios.

Ray, who has been strongly involved in the publication of a monthly children's magazine, *Sandesh*, since 1960 and has written several novels for youngsters, knows how to hold their attention—by filling the screen with wonderful characters and locales, transmitting a real feel for adventure in the process.

Soumitra Chatterjee and Siddhartha Chatterjee on location. Photograph by Sandip Ray

The Golden Fortress is about boy Mukul, who stays up at night drawing pictures of people and places he's never seen. With the help of a parapsychologist, it's determined that he's recalling events from a former life. The doctor takes Mukul on a journey from Calcutta to Rajastan in an attempt to locate a certain golden fortress the boy dreams about where he says jewels are kept. Two con men read about the trip in the paper, convincingly intercept and befriend Mukul, while a private eye and his teenage assistant, wise to their scheme, follow their trail.

Though the film runs a bit long, there is no padding, nor is there any of the forced slapstick and soft violence that dominate many American children's films. Rather, Ray relies on his storytelling talents and rich characterizations. The performers are quite good and sometimes very funny. The film is also beautifully photographed. It was shown at the 1975 Teheran Children's Festival.

AWARDS AND RECOGNITION

List of various International and National awards won by *Sonar Kella*

1. Winner of the Government of West Bengal Award for Best Film and Best Director, 1974
2. Golden Statue for the 'Best Live Feature Film', Tenth Teheran International Festival of Films for Children and Young Adults, 1975
3. Nominee for Best Feature Film for Gold Hugo Award, Chicago International Film Festival, 1975
4. Winner of various awards at the 22nd National Film Festival, New Delhi, 1975
    - Golden Lotus Award for Best Direction
    - Silver Lotus Award for Best Screenplay
    - Regional Award for Best Feature Film in Bengali
    - National Film award for Best Cinematography (awarded to Soumendu Ray)
    - National Film Award for Best Child Artist (awarded to Kushal Chakraborty)

Award for the Best Bengali Film

SONAR KELLA

Producer: **Information and Public Relations Department, Government of West Bengal.**

Director: **Satyajit Ray**

THE Rajat Kamal Award for the Best Bengali Film of 1974 goes to SONAR KELLA produced by the Information and Public Relations Department of the Government of Bengal and directed by Satyajit Ray.

Shri Satyajit Ray, our most distinguished film maker, stands in a class by himself. His first feature film, Pather Panchali, had the unique distinction of winning the largest number of international honours ever received in the history of world cinema. He is also the only film maker to have received the Raymon Magsaysay Award which he won in 1967.

Shri Ray's films have won numerous prizes and awards over the years, both nationally and internationally. Last year's National Award for the Best Bengali film was also won by him for Ashani Sanket.

Honours have been showered on Shri Satyajit Ray all over the world. Earlier this year, the prestigious British Federation of Film Societies named him as the most distinguished international director in the last half century.

The Information and Public Relations Department of the Government of West Bengal, producer of Sonar Kella, the Best Bengali Film of 1974, receives a Rajat Kamal, a cash prize of Rs. 10,000 and a Certificate.

Shri Satyajit Ray, the film's director, receives a Rajat Kamal, and a Certificate.

Shri Soumitra Chatterjee
Male lead player, receives a medallion.

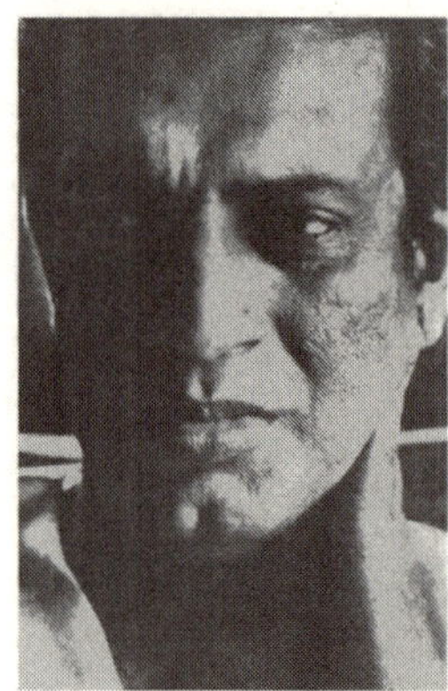

Award for Excellence in Direction

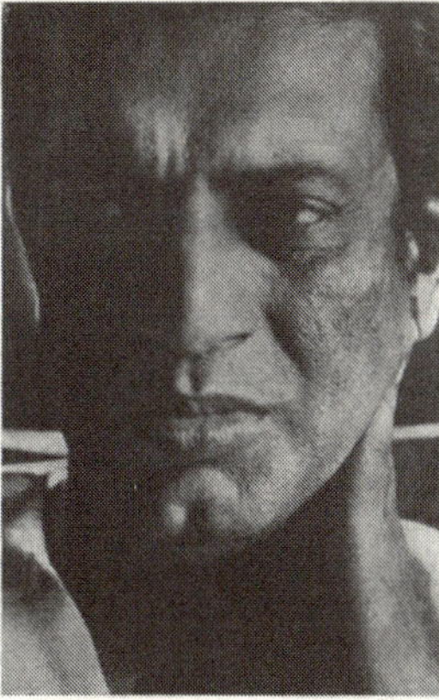

Satyajit Ray
Film: SONAR KELLA

Winner of the Best Bengali Film Award of 1974.

THE Rajat Kamal for Excellence in Direction goes to Shri Satyajit Ray for the award winning Bengali Film SONAR KELLA.
Shri Satyajit Ray, Director of Sonar Kella, receives a Rajat Kamal, a cash prize of Rs. 20,000 and a Certificate.

Award for Excellence in Cinematography (Colour)

Soumendu Roy
Film: SONAR KELLA

Winner of the Best Bengali Film of 1974.

THE Rajat Kamal for Excellence in Cinematography (colour) goes to Soumendu Roy for the award-winning Bengali film, Sonar Kella. This is the second consecutive year in which Shri Soumendu Roy has received this award. Last year, he won it for his colour photography in ASHANI SANKET.
Shri Soumendu Roy began his career in 1954 as a camera apprentice in Technicians Studios, Calcutta under Ramananda Sen Gupta.
Later, he assisted Shri Subrata Mitra and then worked independently as Cameraman on Satyajit Ray's films, Tagore and Teen Kanya. He has since been Cameraman for a series of Ray films. These include Abhijan, Kapurush-o-Mahapurush, Chiria Khana, Aranyer Din Ratre and Simabadha.
In 1967, Shri Soumendu Roy represented the country's Eastern Zone as a Technician Delegate in the U.S.S.R. Last year, he was invited to the International Cinematographers' Conference in Los Angeles, U.S.A.
Shri Soumendu Roy, Cinematographer of Sonar Kella, receives a Rajat Kamal, a cash prize of Rs. 5,000 and a Certificate.

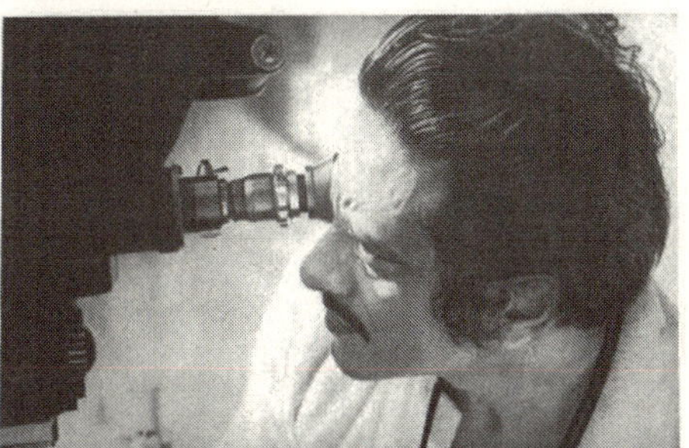

Award for the Best Screen Play of 1974

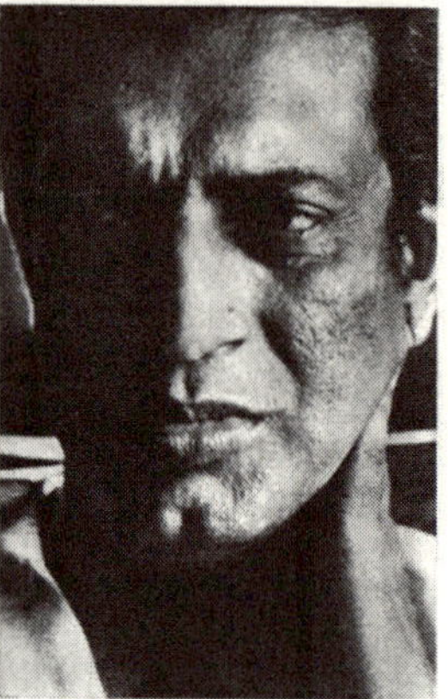

Satyajit Ray
Film: SONAR KELLA
Winner of Best Bengali Film Award for 1974.

THE Rajat Kamal Award for the Best Screen Play of the year goes to Satyajit Ray for scripting of the Bengali film SONAR KELLA Shri Satyajit Ray receives, for the Best Screen Play of the year in Sonar Kella, a Rajat Kamal, a cash prize of Rs. 10,000 and a Certificate.

Award for the Best Child Actor

Master Kushal Chakraborty
Film: SONAR KELLA
Winner of the Best Bengali Feature Film of 1974.

THE Rajat Kamal Award for the Best Child Actor goes to Master Kushal Chakraborty for his performance in Sonar Kella. Eight-year old, Kushal is a class III student at Uttarayan of Birati near Calcutta. Since the age of five, he has contributed pictures and sketches to magazines and newspapers. Some of these have been published by Anand Mala and Pat Tari, the children's supplements of Ananda Bazar and Jugantar Patrika. He is also the author of "Amar Chhabi Tomar Chhara", a collection of pictures illustrating poems by eminent poets of Bengal. These caught the attention of Satyajit Ray who starred Kushal in Sonar Kella. Kushal is also interested in coin and stamp collecting. Master Kushal Chakraborty, the Best Child Actor receives for his performance in Sonar Kella a Rajat Kamal, a cash prize of Rs. 5,000 and a Certificate.

A LABOUR OF LOVE

This unique visual schedule prepared by Satyajit Ray, is an exemplary piece of work showcasing Ray's meticulous planning and his infallible eye for detail. He used a large cartridge paper and pinned it on a board to prepare it with great care. The entire film was primarily split into ten sequences, each covering several scenes. The deft planning of sequences nos. 5 to 10 covering the entire outdoor shoot in Rajasthan has been included in this schedule. The left side panel in the sheet indicates the date and location. The daily shooting plan was divided into three sections—'Morning', 'Afternoon' and 'Evening'. Each section contained very brief description of the scenes along with the names of the actors involved. A special note titled 'Talkie' or 'Silent' was also mentioned in order to indicate if the referred scene demanded sound recording.

Starting date 27 January 1973.

27 January

Morning: Leave Howrah at 9.35 am by Toofan Express.

28 January

Morning: Between Kanpur and Fetehpur
Sequence 5 (Silent) Felu + Tapesh (2 short scenes)

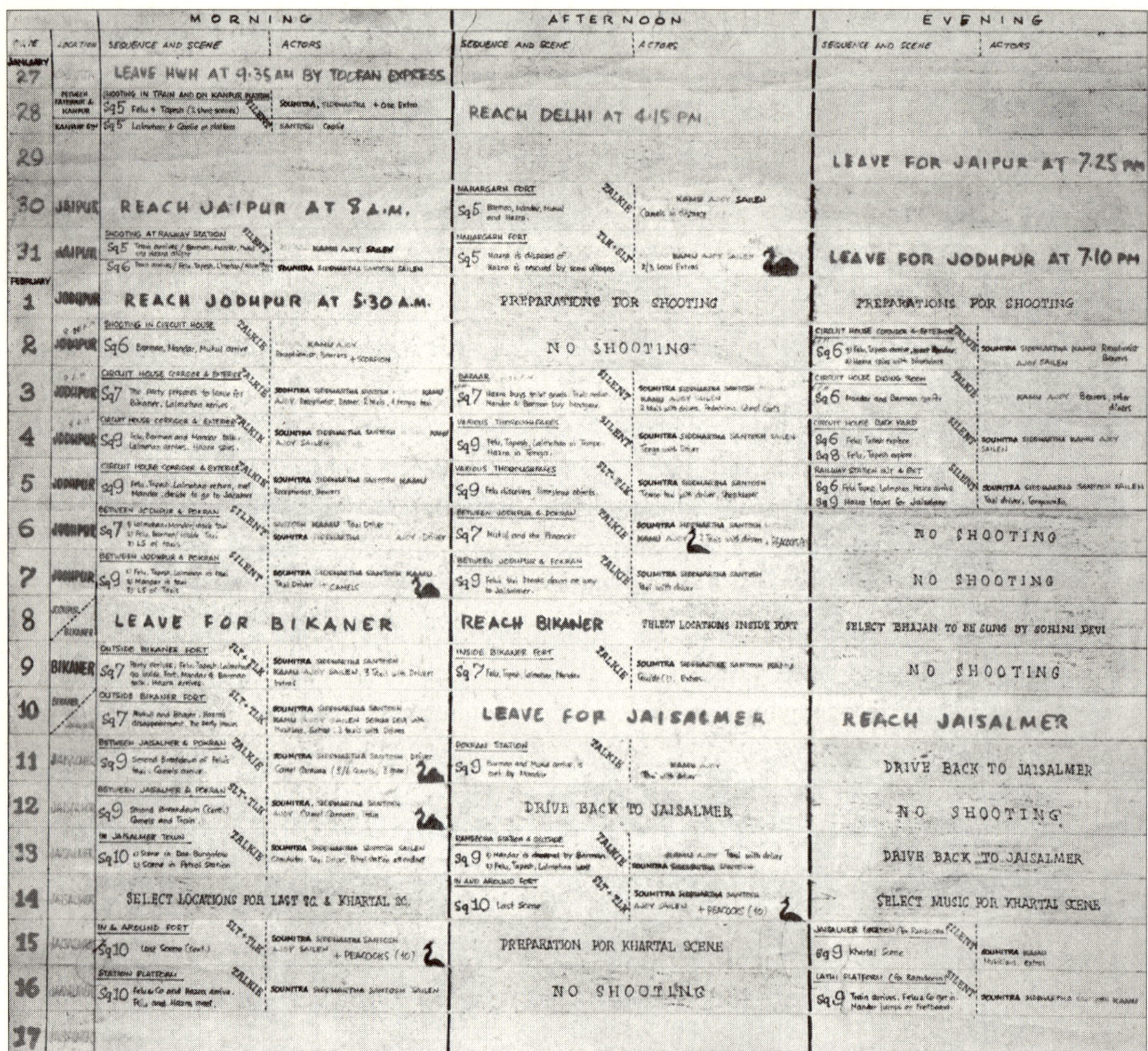

DATE	LOCATION	MORNING: SEQUENCE AND SCENE	MORNING: ACTORS	AFTERNOON: SEQUENCE AND SCENE	AFTERNOON: ACTORS	EVENING: SEQUENCE AND SCENE	EVENING: ACTORS
JANUARY 27	[illegible]	LEAVE HWH AT 9.35 AM BY TOOFAN EXPRESS					
28	[illegible] KANPUR / KANPUR STN	SHOOTING IN TRAIN AND ON KANPUR PLATFORM (SILENT) Sq5 Felu + Topshe (3 short scenes); Sq5 Lalmohan & Coolie on platform	SOUMITRA, SIDDHARTHA + One Extra; SANTOSH Coolie	REACH DELHI AT 4.15 PM			
29						LEAVE FOR JAIPUR AT 7.25 PM	
30	JAIPUR	REACH JAIPUR AT 8 A.M.		NAHARGARH FORT (TALKIE) Sq5 Barman, Mandar, Mukul and Hazra.	KAMU AJOY SAILEN Camels in [illegible]		
31	JAIPUR	SHOOTING AT RAILWAY STATION (SILENT) Sq5 Train arrives / Barman, Mandar, Mukul … ; Sq6 Train arrives / Felu, Topshe, Lalmohan …	KAMU AJOY SAILEN; SOUMITRA SIDDHARTHA SANTOSH SAILEN	NAHARGARH FORT (TLK+SLT) Sq5 Hazra is disposed of. Hazra is rescued by some villagers	KAMU AJOY SAILEN 2/3 local Extras	LEAVE FOR JODHPUR AT 7.10 PM	
FEBRUARY 1	JODHPUR	REACH JODHPUR AT 5.30 A.M.		PREPARATIONS FOR SHOOTING		PREPARATIONS FOR SHOOTING	
2	JODHPUR	SHOOTING IN CIRCUIT HOUSE (TALKIE) Sq6 Barman, Mandar, Mukul arrive	KAMU AJOY Receptionist, Bearers + SCORPION	NO SHOOTING		CIRCUIT HOUSE CORRIDOR & EXTERIOR (TALKIE) Sq6 1) Felu, Topshe arrive, meet Mandar 2) Hazra …	SOUMITRA SIDDHARTHA KAMU AJOY SAILEN Receptionist Bearers
3	JODHPUR	CIRCUIT HOUSE CORRIDOR & EXTERIOR (TALKIE) Sq7 The party prepares to leave for Bikaner. Lalmohan arrives	SOUMITRA SIDDHARTHA SANTOSH … KAMU AJOY Receptionist, Bearer, 2 taxis, 4 tempo …	BAZAAR (SILENT) Sq7 Hazra buys … Mandar & Barman buy …	SOUMITRA SIDDHARTHA SANTOSH … KAMU AJOY SAILEN 2 taxis with drivers, Pedestrians …	CIRCUIT HOUSE DINING ROOM (TALKIE) Sq6 Mandar and Barman …	KAMU AJOY Bearers, other diners
4	JODHPUR	CIRCUIT HOUSE CORRIDOR & EXTERIOR (TALKIE) Sq8 Felu, Barman and Mandar talk. Lalmohan arrives. Hazra spies.	SOUMITRA SIDDHARTHA SANTOSH … KAMU AJOY SAILEN	VARIOUS THOROUGHFARES (SILENT) Sq9 Felu, Topshe, Lalmohan in Tempo. Hazra in Tempo.	SOUMITRA SIDDHARTHA SANTOSH SAILEN Tempo with Driver	CIRCUIT HOUSE BACK YARD (SILENT) Sq6 Felu, Topshe explore; Sq8 Felu, Topshe explore	SOUMITRA SIDDHARTHA KAMU AJOY SAILEN
5	JODHPUR	CIRCUIT HOUSE CORRIDOR & EXTERIOR (TALKIE) Sq9 Felu, Topshe, Lalmohan return, meet Mandar, decide to go to Jaisalmer	SOUMITRA SIDDHARTHA SANTOSH KAMU Receptionist, Bearers	VARIOUS THOROUGHFARES (SLT+TLK) Sq9 Felu discovers … objects.	SOUMITRA SIDDHARTHA SANTOSH Tempo taxi with driver, Shopkeeper	RAILWAY STATION EXT & INT (SILENT) Sq6 Felu Topshe Lalmohan Hazra arrive; Sq9 Hazra leaves for Jaisalmer	SOUMITRA SIDDHARTHA SANTOSH SAILEN Taxi driver, …
6	JODHPUR	BETWEEN JODHPUR & POKRAN (SILENT) Sq7 1) Lalmohan, Mandar inside Taxi 2) Felu, Barman inside Taxi 3) LS of taxis	SANTOSH KAMU Taxi Driver; SOUMITRA SIDDHARTHA … AJOY Driver	BETWEEN JODHPUR & POKRAN (TALKIE) Sq7 Mukul and the Peacocks	SOUMITRA SIDDHARTHA SANTOSH … KAMU AJOY 2 Taxis with drivers, Peacocks	NO SHOOTING	
7	JODHPUR	BETWEEN JODHPUR & POKRAN (SILENT) Sq9 1) Felu, Topshe, Lalmohan in taxi 2) Mandar in taxi 3) LS of Taxis	SOUMITRA SIDDHARTHA SANTOSH KAMU Taxi Driver + CAMELS	BETWEEN JODHPUR & POKRAN (TALKIE) Sq9 Felu's taxi breaks down on way to Jaisalmer.	SOUMITRA SIDDHARTHA SANTOSH Taxi with driver	NO SHOOTING	
8	JODHPUR / BIKANER	LEAVE FOR BIKANER		REACH BIKANER	SELECT LOCATIONS INSIDE FORT	SELECT BHAJAN TO BE SUNG BY SOHINI DEVI	
9	BIKANER	OUTSIDE BIKANER FORT (SLT+TLK) Sq7 Party arrives, Felu, Topshe, Lalmohan go inside Fort, Mandar & Barman talk. Hazra arrives	SOUMITRA SIDDHARTHA SANTOSH KAMU AJOY SAILEN, 3 Taxis with Drivers …	INSIDE BIKANER FORT (TALKIE) Sq7 Felu, Topshe, Lalmohan, Mandar	SOUMITRA SIDDHARTHA SANTOSH KAMU Guide(?), Extras	NO SHOOTING	
10	BIKANER / JAISALMER	OUTSIDE BIKANER FORT (SLT+TLK) Sq7 Mukul and Bhagat, Hazra's disappearance. The party leaves	SOUMITRA SIDDHARTHA SANTOSH KAMU AJOY SAILEN … 3 taxis with Drivers	LEAVE FOR JAISALMER		REACH JAISALMER	
11	JAISALMER	BETWEEN JAISALMER & POKRAN (TALKIE) Sq9 Second Breakdown of Felu's taxi. Camels arrive.	SOUMITRA SIDDHARTHA SANTOSH Driver Camel Owners (5/6 Camels, 3 men)	POKRAN STATION (TALKIE) Sq9 Barman and Mukul arrive, … by Mandar	KAMU AJOY Taxi with driver	DRIVE BACK TO JAISALMER	
12	JAISALMER	BETWEEN JAISALMER & POKRAN (SLT+TLK) Sq9 Second Breakdown (Cont.) Camels and Train	SOUMITRA, SIDDHARTHA SANTOSH AJOY Camel Owners, …	DRIVE BACK TO JAISALMER		NO SHOOTING	
13	JAISALMER	IN JAISALMER TOWN (TALKIE) Sq10 1) Scene in Dak Bungalow 2) Scene in Petrol Station	SOUMITRA SIDDHARTHA SANTOSH SAILEN Chowkidar, Taxi Driver, Petrol station attendant	RAMDEORA STATION & OUTSIDE (TALKIE) Sq9 1) Mandar is … by Barman 2) Felu, Topshe, Lalmohan …	KAMU AJOY Taxi with driver; SOUMITRA SIDDHARTHA SANTOSH	DRIVE BACK TO JAISALMER	
14	JAISALMER	SELECT LOCATIONS FOR LAST SC. & KHARTAL SC.		IN AND AROUND FORT (SLT+TLK) Sq10 Last Scene	SOUMITRA SIDDHARTHA SANTOSH AJOY SAILEN + PEACOCKS (40)	SELECT MUSIC FOR KHARTAL SCENE	
15	JAISALMER	IN & AROUND FORT (SLT+TLK) Sq10 Last Scene (Cont.)	SOUMITRA SIDDHARTHA SANTOSH AJOY SAILEN + PEACOCKS (40)	PREPARATION FOR KHARTAL SCENE		JAISALMER … (SILENT) Sq9 Khartal Scene	SOUMITRA KAMU Musicians, extras
16	JAISALMER	STATION PLATFORM (TALKIE) Sq10 Felu & Co and Hazra arrive. Felu and Hazra meet.	SOUMITRA SIDDHARTHA SANTOSH SAILEN	NO SHOOTING		LATHI PLATFORM (… Ramdeora) (SILENT) Sq9 Train arrives. Felu & Co get in. Mandar jumps on footboard.	SOUMITRA SIDDHARTHA … KAMU
17	JAISALMER						

The schedule prepared by Ray. The colour version is given in the insert.

	Sequence 5 (Silent) Lalmohan + Coolie on the platform.
Afternoon	Reach Delhi at 4.15pm; There was no work in the evening.
29 January	
Morning	No work in Afternoon.
Evening	Leave for Jaipur at 7.25pm.
30 January	
Morning	Reach Jaipur at 8am.
Afternoon	Nahargarh Fort.
	Sequence 5 (Talkie) Barman, Mandar, Mukul and Hazra.
	Camels in distance.
Evening	Rest.
31 January	
Morning	Shooting at Railway Station.
	Sequence 5 (Silent) Train arrives/Barman, Mandar, Mukul and Hazra alight.
	Sequence 5 (Silent) Train arrives/Felu, Tapesh, Lalmohan, Hazra
Afternoon	Nahargarh Fort.
	Sequence 5 (Talk + Silent) Hazra is disposed of. He is rescued by some villagers. List of actors included 2/3 local extras.
Evening	Leave for Jodhpur at 7.10 pm.
1 February	
Morning	Reach Jodhpur at 5.30am.
Afternoon	Preparations for shooting.
Evening	Preparations for shooting.

2 February

Morning 8 am	Shooting in Jodhpur Circuit House. Sequence 6 (Talkie) Barman, Mandar, Mukul arrive. List of actors included Receptionist, Bearers + Scorpion.
Afternoon	No shooting.
Evening	Circuit House Corridor and Exterior. Sequence 6 (Talkie) 1) Felu, Tapesh arrive, meet Mandar 2) Hazra spies with binoculars

3 February

Morning 8am	Jodhpur Circuit House Corridor and Exterior. Sequence 7 (Talkie) The party prepares to leave for Bikaner, Lalmohan arrives.
Afternoon 1.30 pm	Bazaar. Sequence 7 (Silent) Hazra buys toilet sets. Taxi arrives. Mandar and Barman buy headgear.
Evening 6 pm	Circuit House Dining Room. Sequence 7 (Talkie) Mandar and Barman confer.

4 February

Morning 8 am	Jodhpur Circuit House Corridor and Exterior. Sequence 9 (Talkie) Felu, Barman and Mandar talk, Lalmohan arrives. Hazra spies.
Afternoon	Various thoroughfares. Sequence 9 (Silent) Felu, Tapesh, Lalmohan in Tempo. Hazra in Tonga.
Evening	Circuit House backyard. Sequence 6 (Silent) Felu, Tapesh explore. Sequence 8 (Silent) Felu, Tapesh explore.

5 February

Morning	Jodhpur Circuit House Corridor and Exterior.
	Sequence 9 (Talkie) Felu, Tapesh, Lalmohan return, meet Mandar, decide to go to Jaisalmer.
Afternoon	Various thoroughfares.
	Sequence 9 (Silent) Felu discovers limestone objects.
Evening	Railway Station interior and exterior.
	Sequence 6 (Silent) Felu, Tapesh, Lalmohan, Hazra arrive.
	Sequence 9 (Silent) Hazra leaves for Jaisalmer.

6 February

Morning	Between Jodhpur and Pokran.
	Sequence 7 (Silent)
	1) Lalmohan, Mandar/inside taxi.
	2) Felu, Barman/inside taxi.
	3) LS [Long Shot] of taxis.
Afternoon	Between Jodhpur and Pokran.
	Sequence 7 (Talkie) Mukul and the Peacocks.
Evening	No shooting.

7 February

Morning	Between Jodhpur and Pokran.
	Sequence 9 (Silent)
	1) Felu, Tapesh, Lalmohan in taxi.
	2) Mandar in taxi.
	3) LS of taxis.
Afternoon	Between Jodhpur and Pokran.
	Sequence 9 (Talkie) Felu's taxi breaks down on way to Jaisalmer.
Evening	No shooting.

8 February	
Morning	Leave for Bikaner.
Afternoon	Reach Bikaner. Select locations inside fort.
Evening	Select Bhajan to be sung by Sohini Devi.
9 February	
Morning	Outside Bikaner Fort. Sequence 7 (Silent + Talkie) Party arrives. Felu, Tapesh, Lalmohan go inside Fort, Mandar and Barman talk. Hazra arrives.
Afternoon	Inside Bikaner Fort. Sequence 7 (Talkie) Felu, Tapesh, Lalmohan, Mandar. Guide(?)
Evening	No shooting.
10 February	
Morning	Outside Bikaner Fort. Sequence 7 (Silent + Talkie) Mukul and Bhajan. Hazra's disappointment. The party leaves.
Afternoon	Leave for Jaisalmer.
Evening	Reach Jaisalmer.
11 February	
Morning	Between Jaisalmer and Pokran. Sequence 9 (Talkie) Second Breakdown of Felu's taxi. Camels arrive. [List of actors included Camel caravan (5/6 camels, 3 men)].
Afternoon	Pokran Station. Sequence 9 (Talkie): Barman and Mukul arrive, is met by Mandar.
Evening	Drive back to Jaisalmer.

12 February	
Morning	Between Jaisalmer and Pokran. Sequence 9 (Silent + Talkie) Second Breakdown (continued). Camels and Train.
Afternoon	Drive back to Jaisalmer.
Evening	No shooting.
13 February	
Morning	In Jaisalmer Town. Sequence10 (Talkie) 1) Scene in Dak Bungalow. 2) Scene in Petrol Station. [A separate scene was conceived with Felu, Tapesh, Lalmohan, Hazra, Chowkidar, Taxi Driver, Petrol Station attendant—but finally discarded]
Afternoon	Ramdeora Station and Outside. Sequence 9 (Talkie) 1) Mandar is dropped by Barman. 2) Felu, Tapesh, Lalmohan wait.
Evening	Drive back to Jaisalmer.
14 February	
Morning	Select locations for Last Scene. Khartal scene.
Afternoon	In and around Fort; Sequence 10 (Silent + Talkie) Last scene.
Evening	Select music for Khartal scene.
15 February	
Morning	In and around Jaisalmer Fort. Sequence 10 (Silent + Talkie) Last scene (continued)

Afternoon	Preparation for Khartal Scene.
Evening	Jaisalmer location (for Ramdeora).
	Sequence 9 (Silent) Khartal Scene.

16 February

Morning	Jaisalmer Station Platform.
	Sequence 10 (Talkie) Felu and Co and Hazra arrive.
	Felu and Hazra meet.
Afternoon	No shooting.
Evening	Lathi Platform (for Ramdeora).
	Sequence 9 (Silent) Train arrives. Felu and Co. get in.
	Mandar jumps on footboard.

The schedule comes to an end with this scene. The readers can well imagine the amount of preparedness needed to plan such an elaborate outdoor shoot in advance. The way Ray used different font styles and colour tones to distinguish between different sections and thumbnail camels to symbolize a camel scene, this schedule is a testament of the whole-hearted involvement and passion the director had for the entire creative process of the film.

SOCIETY FOR THE PRESERVATION OF SATYAJIT RAY ARCHIVES

www.satyajitrayworld.org

PRESERVING A PRICELESS LEGACY

Sometime after the demise of Satyajit Ray, a number of actors and public personalities—Amitabh Bachchan and the late Ismail Merchant being among them—teamed up to form what is today the Society for the Preservation of Satyajit Ray Archives. Popularly known as Satyajit Ray Society, it was founded in 1994 with the objective of restoring and preserving the priceless legacies left by the master director as also of disseminating his work worldwide.

RAY RESTORATION

When Ray breathed his last in 1992, negatives and prints of many of his films, especially those of his early classics, were in a precarious state. David H. Shepard, a noted film preservationist in California, came to India to examine the original negatives of the Ray films. He found the negatives of eighteen of his films in 'tatters'. Restoration of Ray films was the Society's primary concern at the time. It went into a tie-up with the Los Angeles based Academy of Motion Picture Arts and Sciences, the hallowed institution which had conferred the Oscar for Lifetime Achievement on Ray.

RAY ARCHIVES

Apart from his films, Ray left behind an astonishingly wide artistic universe comprising scripts, storyboards, posters, set, costume and book jacket designs, literary manuscripts, illustrations, music notations, advertisement artworks and so on. The Society has arguably the largest and most authentic archive on Ray in its custody. A veritable treasure trove, the Ray paper archive contains almost the entire creative output of his many-faceted genius. A large part of Ray's paper legacy was restored under the supervision of Mike Wheeler, Senior Conservator (Paper Preservation) at the Victoria-Albert Museum, London, and is housed in Ray's family home in Kolkata. The large personal library that Ray left and his personal effects are also being carefully preserved.

PUBLISHING RAY BOOKS

As part of the dissemination campaign, the Society has begun to publish books by Ray. It brought out *Deep Focus: Reflection on Cinema*, a collection of long-lost essays by Ray, in December 2011, in collaboration with HarperCollins India. The Society published, jointly with HarperCollins India, *Satyajit Ray's Ravi Shankar*, a facsimile edition of the visual script that the master director drew for his intended film on the sitar maestro. The Society also brought out *Probandho Sangroho*, a collection of Bengali essays by Ray, jointly with Ananda Publishers Pvt. Ltd. on 1 May 2015. Next, the Society brought out yet another book in collaboration with HarperCollins India—*The Pather Panchali Sketchbook*, which is a facsimile of the visual storyboard that Ray created for his maiden film. The last publication, which too is the outcome of the joint collaboration between the Society and HarperCollins India, is *Travails with the Alien*. The book includes Ray's script for *The Alien*, a film which he wanted to make in Hollywood but failed to do. The book was launched by Sharmila Tagore at a ceremony that the Society organized on 28 April 2018 to mark the ninety-seventh birth anniversary of Satyajit Ray. Now the Ray Society has tied up with Penguin Random House India to create the 'Penguin Ray Library' which will strive to bring out the entire oeuvre of writings created by the master. Satyajit Ray has a long association with Penguin India and the coming together of the Society with Penguin

Random House is a homecoming of sorts. Two books full of archival materials—*3 Rays* and *Ray Miscellany*—have been published as part of this initiative in 2021 and 2022 respectively.

RAY MEMORIAL LECTURES

The Society has been organizing lectures dedicated to Ray's memory by distinguished film personalities for quite a few years. Javed Akhtar gave the first lecture in 2009, followed by Shyam Benegal (2012) and Naseeruddin Shah (2014). Soumitra Chatterjee delivered the next lecture on the eve of Ray's ninety-fourth birth anniversary on 1 May 2015, and Aparna Sen on 1 May 2017. Sharmila Tagore delivered the lecture on 28 April 2018. In 2019, Penguin Random House India collaborated with the society to create the Annual Penguin Ray Lecture Series. On that occasion, Tarun Majumdar gave a lecture on 27 April 2019. On 1 May 2023, the society organized a tête-à-tête with Jaya Bachchan regarding her debut in *Mahanagar* while on 1 May 2024 there was a similar programme involving the surviving members of the cast of *Sonar Kella*.

EXHIBITIONS, SEMINARS AND FILM SHOWS

The Society has arranged quite a number of exhibitions of Ray's artworks as also festivals of his films and seminars on his work, at home and abroad. Some of the places where such shows and film retrospectives have taken place are Kolkata, Mumbai, Delhi, Hyderabad, Bangalore, Toronto, Valladolid, San Francisco, London and Amsterdam. The Society organized its largest seminar (on *Pather Panchali*) in August 2015 in Kolkata. The participants were Sharmila Tagore, Aparna Sen, Dibakar Banerjee, Shoojit Sircar, Nandita Das, Sujoy Ghosh, Suman Mukhopadhyay and Dileep Padgaonkar. The seminar was moderated by Dhritiman Chaterji. In 2019, the society organized an exhibition to commemorate fifty years of *Goopy Gyne Bagha Byne* at Kolkata. In 2023 and 2024, the society screened the restored version of *Mahanagar* and *Sonar Kella* respectively to packed audience in Nandan, Kolkata.

ACKNOWLEDGEMENTS

Abhijit Sukul

Ananda Publishers Pvt. Ltd.

Allied Publishers

Arunava Sinha

Bichitropotra Granthana Vibhagha

www.fatafatee.co.in

Indrani Majumder

Lolita Ray

Neeraj Nath

Saloni Mital

Souradeep Ray

Ray guiding Kushal Chakraborty. Photograph by Sandip Ray

Scan QR code to access the
Penguin Random House India website